THE CHANCE AGAIN

ISBN 978-0-578-93510-2

The Chance Again

William J. Conway

I am grateful in a dozen ways to my editor, Laurie Scheer, who guided me through the process, and to those of you who have stuck with me and prolonged the challenge. You know who you are. My daughters, Elizabeth and Amy, provided technical and personal support without which none of this would have happened.

Content Advisory

This book contains offensive language, including racial slurs that are part of an effort to retain the integrity of the story herein. Racist language was wrong during the time the story takes place and it is wrong today. The author and publisher do not condone, support, or promote the use of racist language in any way.

"The key is not to discover when it comes time to die that you never lived."

Henry David Thoreau, *Walden*

CONTENTS

ARRIVAL

"Dwells in me still my irksome memory
Which both to keep and lose grieves equally."

John Donne, *Sappho to Philaenis*

In July, 1991, Oliver Angus Lockett wears a grey suit jacket soaked through with New Orleans' humidity as he parks his state car at the airport. Earlier he's a staff face when he apologizes for the governor who knows they're worth bothering about but wants no part of a third pain in the ass meeting with a buyer's club of local politicians jockeying for Super Dome money while they suck up or nag with a litany of personal projects: a church parking lot, a new high school score board, a road paved to a new camp.

It's Friday, the city shuts down at noon. By now, they're into their second drink at a favorite French Quarter watering hole, *le laissez le bon temps rouler*. Lockett heads for the Oyster Bar. In two hours, he'll be on a Northwest flight for a week of vacation in Wisconsin. He takes a seat next to the attractive woman who's better looking than her photos. He loosens his red Hermes tie with the small animal designs. They watch the white-haired bartender joke and finesse customers with cocktails. She sips a Stella Artois. He belts his Abita and orders a second. He can't remember her name. He introduces himself. He tells her the bartender is called Storyteller. He waits a minute. He asks how long before her flight. "Two hours," she says. "Tell me, who are you?"

"I'm with the governor's office."

"No, not what you do, who are you?"

Gloria Steinem is serious.

11

DEPARTURE

"What was taking place in him was completely unfamiliar, new, sudden, never before experienced. Not that he understood it, but he clearly sensed, with all the power of sensation, that it was no longer possible for him..."

Fyodor Dostoevsky, *Crime and Punishment*

What do you do with that? Where do you go for clues? How do you reduce to "who are you?" How do you even remember experiences or relationships that changed you? How do you shape an answer that's honest and complete? It probably won't be either and she'll smoke out anything that's too cute or political.

Lockett pictured Grand Lac, a thousand miles west of Montreal, mid-afternoon, the second Saturday in June, 1954, his first summer at being young the way other boys were young.

He couldn't remember who made the introduction, but he remembered the soft handshake. Jack Clear was a year older, black hair, copper skin, mixed blood Ojibwa on his father's side. Archambeau was called Chief, Rabideaux was Tonto, Clear was Clear. Somebody said he was Santa in the orphanage with the girls.

"You live on twenty first," he said, "right? I gave Foley's girl a ride home from the Bandstand last night, twenty first, a block off Hammond. He didn't show. She's a cheerleader, blond, really smart. Lives that close, you should meet her. They let you dance?"

The idea of a girl caught Lockett off guard. He had kissed Rosie but that wasn't on purpose. He'd never held a girl's hand, never had a date, didn't have a car. Clear had this funny way of knowing things, sometimes before they happened. He must know he didn't dance.

Lockett tightened the strings on the blue canvas apron that kept Evening Chronicle newspaper ink off their clothes. He cleared his throat.

"Hardly," he said.

Clear stared away. Sometimes he looked that way, like he was one place and everybody was someplace else.

Lockett imagined his neighborhood, a cheerleader named Delores a few years earlier but she graduated. If Clear was right, and the girl was that cute, why didn't he ask her out? And Bobby Foley wasn't smart enough to know he couldn't afford to stiff a cute girl. The cheerleader didn't add up. That was the world Lockett lived in, a new world filled with gaps like that.

Fitzgibbons stood on the other side of Clear. He was tall. His hair looked like an upside down shoe brush from too much butch wax. He leaned behind Clear and told Lockett to pick an ugly girl because she'd be more grateful. And pretty girls were lousy kissers.

Clear gave Fitz a look and told him to leave Lockett alone. He put a hand on Lockett's shoulder.

"Be careful, you're the new cherry. Fitz wants to do more than kiss you. Pretty girls fuck that up."

Fitz shoved Clear and laughed.

"Never should have let your people off the reservation."

The rest of the mail room crew broke up. Clear never blinked. He looped his thumbs in his pants pockets and stared at Fitz.

"We are all colored by the same sun," he said, "but my people know how to live."

That pretty much summed up who Clear was. He didn't seem to want or need anything from anybody, as if, in some Ojibwa way, he had been places and done things that nobody knew about.

All that was true a few weeks after Clear bought the two year old light blue Ford hardtop and painted it black. He chopped off the door handles and the chrome. Then he lowered it and brought it to a shop that customized insides with leather tucks and rolls like California cars. He added Hollywood mufflers and Fitz called it "sinister." Everybody agreed, Clear was the coolest driver with the coolest car.

It may have been too romantic, but the first ten days in the mail room had seemed almost poetic. Not the kind of poetry you think about between two people who can't stand being apart, but Lockett had traded the company of committed seminarians for a dozen young men tweaking who they wanted to be every day.

Like the three high school drop outs who wrapped cigarette packs in white tee shirt sleeves and peppered their conversations with four letter words as if they were basic to the English language. And Arnie, who was a senior with a mop of blond hair. He got his job because Fitz thought Arnie was cute and Fitz's father was the foreman.

Duschesne was another senior. He came early for work and said "yes sir" and "no sir" to the foreman. He didn't drink or smoke. He dressed in pressed chinos and preppy button-down shirts, and rolled his sleeves to the elbows. His father inherited the family funeral home and everybody expected Duschesne to go to mortuary school until he and a friend propped a corpse upright in the front seat of a hearse during a blizzard and drove to a slumber party to shock the girls. On the way back, the hearse slid into a snow bank in front of a light pole and cracked the radiator. The police tried to keep it quiet, but it got out and everybody imagined a father or mother in the front seat. The mortuary went under. Duschesne's father and the foreman were friends. Lockett figured that's how Duschesne got hired.

Fats Lund struggled with his weight and a round oily face like it hadn't seen a washcloth in a week. His job was the easiest. The conveyor from the pressroom turned every fiftieth paper sideways. All Fats had to do was set the bunch of fifties on the table in front of Clear and Lockett while they counted to make bundles for a hundred paper routes around the city, forty-eight, eighty-seven etc. Somebody said Fats worked alone because he smelled bad. Somebody else said there wasn't enough space for him to work next to someone. A few said it was more than that. But he was Clear's friend and that's how he kept the job.

Lockett saw Fat's sister Julia for the first time in the back of their father's old green Plymouth, when Fat's car wouldn't start and his father drove him to work. Something went tight in the back of Lockett's throat when Fitz called her "little Fats" because she was almost as big and had the same acne. That kind of talk wouldn't have happened with the priests.

All Lockett knew about his job was what Fitz told him.

The foreman had tended bar for his father and clipped the till for two hundred dollars, during his divorce. Lockett's father caught him. He paid back about half the two hundred before Lockett's father threatened him for the rest. He said he didn't have it. Lockett's father told him, "Then put the kid to work." That was the way his father saw a lot of things when he was drinking. Even the foreman said nobody tested him. The summer job ended up being the foreman's way to repay the last hundred.

Every day, Lockett listened to unfamiliar talk about girls and drinking and cars, shallow stuff with words like nooky and shag and tail. He cut the exaggerations in half and weeded out the drama about girls. What they said wasn't exactly a lie. To tell a lie, you had to know the truth. But when they got going, they talked in monosyllables and jerky sentences and everything seemed measured against their cars and girls and best drinking. Cars meant freedom and power. Girls meant manhood and control. In Grand Lac, drinking was basic to ideas like that and most everything else. They never said it, but cars came first.

Sometimes, Lockett felt tested to see how he fit in. Like when one of the drop outs told an old story about drinking five beers when his car was in the shop before walking Fern Schultz home after *The Creature From the Black Lagoon*. He said he couldn't hold it anymore and Fern grabbed his penis and wrote her name in the snow. "Slowly," the guy said. Fitz reminded him that Fern had a sister named Marguerite and asked if the longer name would have changed the story.

Lockett stayed quiet during stories like that, especially the ones that drifted between French kissing and getting laid or not getting laid. He cringed at details like searching inside a girl's blouse. Even creepier was the idea of a girl putting her tongue in a guy's mouth. He tried not to think about details that were more sinful, and how dark and unforgiving God's response could be. He had just come from two years of listening and curiosity and fear about things like that. He assumed he would sort it out.

The third Saturday, Fitz asked Lockett if he wanted a beer after work. Fitz was coarse but it was either that or another Saturday night at home. Fitz bought two quarts of Schlitz at the Nottingham grocery and Lockett drank for the first time.

Fitz told a story about testing to find out if he was gay or straight.

"I'm not one thing or the other particularly," he said.

A month earlier, he had lied to a guy named McVitie about plans for the weekend. He was on the porch swing with McVitie's girlfriend at Eau Claire Lakes when he spotted McVitie coming down the hill. He bolted for his old Mercury station wagon and buried the accelerator to the floor. McVitie chased him for fifteen miles on dirt roads firing the long barreled .22 pistol he used to shoot rats at the city dump. He was still shooting when he missed a curve off highway 27 and rolled his Olds and spent three days in the hospital.

"Last thing I saw in my mirror was McVitie plowing through poplar trees tearing up that '88," Fitz said.

"Crazy son of a bitch could have killed me."

He rolled his eyes.

"Oh, the messiness of human relationships. As if I'm a rat? It's just too much."

Everyone knew McVitie wasn't exactly normal. He kicked a guy in the mouth during a fight and it cost the guy almost all his teeth. He caught neighborhood cats and dipped them in kerosene during snowstorms. He lit them on fire then threw them off his garage into snow banks and watched them "sizzle down the alley." At sixteen,

Lockett wondered if "testing" tapped into something about sex that he should have felt by then but hadn't.

His world was shaping up like a puzzle with a lot of missing pieces.

A few weeks earlier, he finished his sophomore year at a place nobody in the mailroom had heard of. St. Ignatius was as much a prep school for rich young boys as it was for future priests. Lessons were final: right and wrong, yes and no, good and evil, praise and blame. *The Handbook of Rules* boiled behavior down to learning that celibacy, discipline and growing up could be uncomfortable.

> "If you hear the Sirens song, you have opened
> yourself to new music and new desires and
> already loosened yourself from God. What
> looks like a beginning to you is at the center
> for the girl. Desire is what she sings to. If you
> listen to her voice, you will never have the
> discipline to travel to the place where you
> belong."

The word "Protestant" was never used, but the message made it sound like Sirens had to be Protestant.

Conversations about homosexuals made them even more dangerous. The priests didn't say how, but homosexual was connected to "effeminate" and "corruption."

> "Touching another male is grounds for expulsion,
> except in athletic contests or fighting. Fighting is
> unacceptable but inevitable. Upperclassmen are
> expected to move participants out of buildings.
> Dancing with girls is grounds for expulsion.
> Grades may be reduced for writing without
> specificity such as use of the word 'thing.'"

18

A handful of Lockett's classmates were effeminate but he was sure they couldn't be future priests and homosexual. Fats was effeminate, with a voice like a girl, but he seemed very normal. Fitz was well built and had a deep voice like you'd expect. Maybe he was queer, but people who saw it at company picnics said he was a better dancer than Clear.

Young Mrs. King had graduated from college that spring. She married Jerry King who lived across the alley. Jerry was older and a lot like his mother Henrietta, who wore too much powder and looked like Dorothy's witch. She didn't have the broom, but after Henrietta's husband died, neighbors remembered him every time she wore his blue suede jacket.

"Poor Bruce," they said, "living with that witch."

Her daughter in law began visiting Lockett's mother after the honeymoon but never on Wednesday. She wore large brimmed hats and her tanned breasts filled bright colored, low cut sundresses. Most of the time they talked about baking and shopping and recipes. Sometimes his mother's voice got low when young Mrs. King whispered about Jerry and sleeping together. Whatever Jerry did or didn't do seemed important.

Henrietta visited on Wednesday, which Lockett figured was why young Mrs. King didn't. She parked herself at the small table with the telephone, smoking Chesterfields for three hours. When the phone rang, she answered and listened for five seconds before she handed it to whoever was closest. When she wanted coffee she said something like, "Marie, do you remember the name of the young man from Maple who flew a jet airplane after the war and crashed someplace in Arizona or California or someplace like that, and oh, do you think you could bring me another cup of coffee?" Lockett's mother dropped whatever she was doing and brought Henrietta coffee with cream and two lumps of sugar.

Lockett ignored her, mostly because he thought about a cobra that didn't strike only because it might lose its coffee.

A few minutes before noon, like hitting a switch, Henrietta asked another nonsense question and moved to the dining room table.

"Oh, Marie, do you remember the name of the young man from Holy Rosary who got drafted and went to Korea and won all those medals and got shot just before he was supposed to come home? Well, I'm getting a little hungry. I think I have time for lunch."

She ate quickly and jelly or juice ran down her jaw from the peanut butter and jelly sandwich or the tomato in the BLT. She forgot to wipe her mouth and said the same thing every time.

"Oh my, I think it's time for my nap."

Later, Lockett's mother would say, "I think she wants to be nice." His father would call her an "old scold" and tell stories, like when Henrietta refused to go to her high school's twenty fifth class reunion because Bruce was in a wheelchair after his stroke and she was ashamed to be with him. Lockett wondered if Bruce died trying to please her. But he liked the idea that Henrietta never imagined his thoughts about her thin daughter in law's deep cleavage. Sometimes it made him nervous when he thought young Mrs. King knew.

Early on a Monday, in late June, the dandelions were still wet when he saw young Mrs. King moving half way across the back yard toward him. She stopped and anchored her hand on her hip, posing like a model in an expensive magazine ad. He looked away at two baby rabbits in the clover patch at the far corner of the lawn. She smiled and said good morning. What she almost whispered sounded like something she couldn't say when someone else was around.

"You know Oliver, Jerry travels all week and Henrietta works in Duluth most days. You can come over anytime."

She was married and Catholic and too old to flirt, but his neck got hot. He blushed. In some ways it was fuzzy. In others ways it was obvious. Either way, she was checking.

He smiled and nodded and said, "Thank you." He saw his mother shake her head in the kitchen window. Nothing ever happened, she never mentioned it. Later he wondered what he would do if he was wrong about young Mrs. King being too old and Catholic and married and if any of it had to do with Jerry.

That summer, lightening bugs and the smell of lilacs around his yard reminded Lockett of girls who smiled that day. Strange feelings started like a small animal building something in his body. Father Mullan had set ten minute appointments for every freshman in his office where he explained that nocturnal emissions weren't a sin. Except for pistols and stamens in biology, that was as close as Lockett had been to sex. And that was a year earlier. Lockett could only guess what his mother thought when she washed his pajamas.

The week before the Fourth of July, the Bandstand moved twenty miles south to the village pavilion at Lake Nebagamon. Saturday nights, Lockett drank beer with Clear and dozens of other underage boys in gravel parking lots outside places like the Gopher Hole where the owner looked like Paladin on the television show. Around ten thirty, everybody left for the dance and what he knew would be an absurd number of girl's suntanned bodies. No matter how comfortable he felt at the bars, or how attractive the girls were, every night ended up pushing against something the priests warned about.

After the third Saturday, Clear seemed to have the answer before he asked Lockett if any of it surprised him.

"Yes," Lockett said, "different. How about you?"

Clear thought for a few seconds.

"My people say all music tells stories."

He started his car. He bit his lip and loosened his grip on the steering wheel. He was sure the county cops around Nebagamon knew about his mufflers. He asked Lockett to drive and said they wouldn't ticket him because it wasn't his car. The surprise sank in. The best part of Lockett's evening was ahead.

A half hour later, Lockett slowed for the curve just south of the city limits. Clear hunched over with his head in his hands. He cried for at least a minute before he looked up and tried to smile.

"I never knew my dad," he said. "I know I was born on Nova Scotia. I think we were happy there. My mother would look at him and then me and smile. On walks, she talked about how we would move here and find the same spirits around Grand Lac, and how I would know them. She said my father knew something about me that made him sad, but he never told her. He disappeared when we were on one of the walks. Later she told me a story that he had told her."

"She said when he was a little boy, he walked along the Atlantic after a big storm. He stopped every few steps and picked up a starfish that washed up. He tossed it back. An old white man came toward him and told him there were too many and what he was doing wouldn't make a difference. My dad bent over and threw another starfish back. 'It does to that one,' he told the old man."

"That's the way I want to remember him. Life is too short."

The last part sounded prophetic. The scary part was Clear always knew. Lockett drove slower.

A week later, he wrote the letter.

"This is to inform you that I will not be returning to St. Ignatius."

In a way, there was more to say and he was hiding. But he thought about Thomas Merton's lessons when he moved into a different world and discovered who he was beyond the discipline and rituals of the monastery. Maybe every time anything important stopped, something else started. That's what he hoped.

Four days later, Father Mullan called. His words sounded somewhere between warnings and threats. He told Lockett he had "a sacred vocation," that God had called him to further his kingdom, and he might be violating God's will. The words reminded Lockett of a caption under some painting. He could see the painting but the words didn't match. He was sure Mullan didn't know what happened or who they were, or who he was.

It seemed like a long time since his first day introductions to the faculty who looked identical in black cassocks. He couldn't remember which one asked what his father did. He said his father was a painter.

"An artist?"

"No, he paints houses."

Whoever said it smiled and walked away. Lockett had an idea about where his grade school classmates lived, which family had a car, what friends ate in their lunches. But it never counted. Humility was how you measured your worth. His mother had taught him that. The priest had added an idea about higher and lower to worth that seemed important. Maybe there was something more to picturing himself from his mother's point of view.

That semester, he read Joyce's *Portrait of an Artist.* He wanted to write like Joyce, to see and know what inspired and moved people. He was nervous about the book as a book report, especially Father Freed's response to Joyce's ideas about guilt, his questions about religion, and marrying a Protestant. He switched to A. J. Cronin's *The Keys to the Kingdom,* a long novel about conflict for a priest.

Freed's hand shook when he returned Lockett's book report in October. He rocked on his toes.

"You should have known better than to choose a book that makes abortion an option. A better choice would have been any biography of a saint. See me after class."

In his office, Freed scolded him and said abortion and extramarital sex should never be seen with sympathy. He said priests were authority figures "who must be portrayed with respect, never as villains." He sighed when he talked about "suffering saints" who thought about their sins with visions of hell. He closed his eyes and talked about "prophesies" and "miraculous healings" and "speaking in tongues." He told Lockett he needed to "cultivate a deeper relationship with God."

The lesson was a darker side of beauty Lockett knew about the church.

The impulse to hitch hike was part escape and part cynicism. He resented ideas that seemed uneven while he might be missing out on something better, somewhere else.

He finished his last exam on the Friday before Christmas, at five o'clock. He paid the dime for the trolley outside the front gate. Twenty-five minutes later, they passed the Milwaukee Road station where the train for Grand Lac would load at seven twenty. He was the last one off when the trolley track ended a mile later. The thirteen-dollar train ticket money would buy gifts. But his parents would be frightened if he wasn't home before the train got there. And a car accident could be worse.

He followed the map for two hundred and fifty miles north. Everything went well until the heavy snow outside Eau Claire. An hour after midnight, an old Dodge stopped. Three Indians laughed when he told them "Grand Lac." The driver said he looked like a "drowned rat." He warned him that all the bars were closed and he might not see another car until morning. But they could get him forty miles further to Chetek. Lockett said okay. The driver lifted his suitcase into the trunk and Lockett got in the back seat next to girl, a few years older. The driver turned and grinned.

"Before we go, you gotta taste our whiskey."

25

The man in the passenger seat passed a half pint of Old Crow. Lockett felt his pulse speed up. His stomach rolled from the metallic taste. Both men laughed.

"Now you gotta kiss Rosie," the driver said.

The girl looked away. Lockett felt the lump in his throat. He regretted trading the quiet campus and the strict rules for a noisy old Dodge where anything was possible. But ending up next to the highway was even worse, especially if they drove off with his suitcase.

The girl leaned over when the men stopped laughing.

"It's alright," she said.

Their lips touched, both men laughed. The last thing Lockett remembered was closing his eyes and the car moving slowly through the storm.

An hour later, the girl nudged him.

"This is as far as we take you," the driver said.

"Knock on the door, somebody's inside, train comes through in a couple hours."

He opened the trunk and extended his hand. The handshake was soft.

"Only a hundred miles to go," he said.

They waited until the depot door opened.

The old western Union telegrapher wore a heavy brown sweater that looked like it had been knitted by hand. He watched as the Dodge pulled away.

"What the hell's going on, they just drop you off?"

Lockett told him about the ride from Eau Claire. The telegrapher shook his head.

"Hitch hiking, Indians, weather like this, your parents know?"

Lockett said no. The telegrapher adjusted his glasses and ran his hand over his bald head. He motioned for

Lockett to come in. He asked his name and where he had started. Lockett gave him his name and told him St. Ignatius and Milwaukee.

"You're gonna be a priest? Should know better, Indians, this time of night? Had to be drunk. How old are you?"

Lockett said fourteen. The telegrapher scowled and pointed to one of two long benches on opposite sides of the wood burning stove. His voice was tense.

"Lay down, over there. Middle of a blizzard. I just can't believe this. Ticket's six twenty five."

He came back a few minutes later with two blankets and the ticket. He took Lockett's jacket and asked him when he had eaten. Lockett was sure he would explode again when he told him noon. But the telegrapher rolled the first blanket and put in under Lockett's head. He said to use the second blanket to cover up. The train would come through at five fifteen and he would wake him.

"Get some sleep."

Lockett paid for the ticket.

"Please mister, don't forget."

The telegrapher stared for five seconds. He cleared his throat as if to say something then shook his head trying to make the best of it. He walked away.

At five fifteen, he touched Lockett's shoulder.

"Train's here, time to go, here's your jacket. I wouldn't do this again if I was you."

Lockett thanked him for letting him stay and for drying his jacket. The telegrapher handed him half a sandwich wrapped in wax paper. This time his voice sounded almost soft.

"Go on son, they're waiting for you. Maybe one day I'll see you on the altar."

Lockett was barely in his seat when he opened the wax paper. The tuna was mixed with mayonnaise, sweet pickles, celery, red onions, garlic and maybe lemon juice on toasted whole wheat bread. The taste was better than any Friday tuna casserole he could remember.

In Grand Lac, his father asked him if he had tipped the conductor. He had, fifty cents, from the seven dollars he had left for Christmas.

Two weeks after Christmas, Father Mack gave the assignment: "Write about a penny, a frog or a leaf. I don't want to see writing like a drunk when you say your subject did this and then he did this and then this was so interesting. Make it unique, use brief sentences. What I want to see is creativity and independent thought, five hundred words."

Lockett rewrote the paper three times before he ran out of synonyms for the word penny. He changed the paper again after he noticed the word *coign* in the dictionary. The last change personalized a traveling penny: in a nun's purse for a month, on a track and run over by a train, added to fourteen pennies for a tap beer at a supper club outside Sheboygan and dropped through a hole in a tourist's pocket in a Parisian subway. He ended the paper with the phrase, "a coin in a *coign.*"

He checked for punctuation, physical descriptions, redundancies, fragmented sentences, and something that happened at the end that really didn't matter. He leaned his head back and smiled.

Mack had a gap in his front teeth, a reputation for tough grading and for returning papers by grades, highest first. He slapped the last paper with the back of his hand and passed it to Lockett. Lockett slid in his seat and stared at the large red F. Mack turned and walked to the front of the room. He fixed on Lockett.

"No freshman can write like that. One should aim at creating without fabricating."

Ever since the anonymous priest the first day, Lockett had notions about humility with different kinds of fairness. Father Freed was still fresh. This time, all the humility in the world might not be enough for his anger. Maybe growing up in Grand Lac had left him with whatever it was, or maybe it was the winters, but fighting back was the way you responded. Not fighting back was weak. For two days he wrestled with an appeal that would test his idea about the paper against Mack's version about what a priest should be. Somewhere between God and the rector, things could be worked out.

He wasn't sure if it was eagerness or fear a week later in Monsignor Chauncey Powers office. Mack sat with his shoulders slumped off to the side of the rector's desk. Lockett hoped the posture meant something good. Powers motioned Lockett to sit down and moved behind his desk.

The new young rector had mingled with students and asked their ideas. Nobody questioned why he became a priest after places like Iwo Jima as a medic with the Marines. But it seemed like he could have done anything he wanted after he came back.

He talked about moral responsibilities and quoted Philippians.

"Forget about what is in the past. Try as hard as you can to reach the goal before you."

He asked Lockett what he would do if he was a teacher and made a grading mistake. Lockett took a deep breath.

"I'd change the grade."

Powers settled back in his chair and asked Mack about the assignment. Mack began speaking. Powers watched Lockett. His head snapped when Mack stood.

"Oliver, are you familiar with the parable of the lost sheep?"

Lockett said yes.

"Are you familiar with the parable of the prodigal son?"

Lockett nodded.

"Have you read the parable of the lost coin?"

Powers stood. He let out a deep breath. His face turned dark.

"Father, we had this discussion. There are no connections."

Lockett leaned in.

"I don't know the parable, Father. I wrote the paper four times. I chose a traveling penny to make a better story. I chose the ending because I thought it was creative. I didn't cheat. The paper is better than an F."

Powers came around his desk and sat on the edge.

"Well, certainly supported with passion."

He looked at Mack.

"Can we agree, Father. Perhaps a B?"

Mack already knew the decision. He shrugged.

Powers pushed off the desk and walked behind it again. He gazed out the window before he sat down.

"How about it then Oliver? Do you agree?"

Lockett nodded. Powers seemed to know the paper deserved an A. He reached across his desk. He shook Lockett's hand, as if wishing none of it had happened. Lockett remembered a Power's sermon about "Restless Faith" a few Sundays earlier.

After that, Lockett's days seemed to unravel. He sensed an increasing skepticism and a separation from priests whose answers used to provide consolation.

The last Friday in October came as one of this special Grand Lac fall mornings. The air was crisp and sweet. The sky was bright. Birds seemed more excited and maples had turned. Lockett saw his breath for the first time on his way to school. The cold morning meant the last days before a hard frost. The real message was about snow.

He glanced up from watching a scrawny yellow cat slink near a lilac hedge. A half block ahead, a cheerleader crossed swinging her arms. Clear hadn't mentioned long legs, but Central's purple and white uniform and the way she swiveled her hips told Lockett she was Clear's cheerleader.

He sucked in a deep breath and walked faster. He stumbled when she turned three blocks later. St. Thomas Aquinas had defined beauty as "wholeness and radiance."

The morning had been good for all the senses.

AND YET, NOT YET

"Does the road wind up-hill all the way?
Yes to the very end.
Will the journey take all day?
From morn to night my friend."

Christina Rossetti, *Up-Hill*

The idea probably came from some poem, but there were times when Lockett linked autumn with dying. Father Lucque had called it *"le point vierge"* what people can learn from what they don't understand.

"I can't translate that," he said, "it's something inaccessible to our mind. But it implies the point where we meet God in a real way."

It wasn't that anything major broke down in the fall of 1954, but Lockett imagined setting out in a small boat and running aground with no help and no one to talk to. Two years in Milwaukee had left him out of step with his new classmates. Especially after the nuns cobbled together a boring vocational menu of typing and bookkeeping with the girls, and three credits of independent reading by himself to replace hours in Latin and philosophy which connected to all the other subjects. He missed the rigor and sometimes the discipline. The most important part of the day came working after school, and a growing friendship with Clear.

By late October, rain knocked down leaves that stuck to car windows. Browns and yellows changed every day. The scent of burning ended. Leaf piles smelled sour. Days grew shorter. Slate colored clouds hid the sky before cold rain and the first big snow when everything went quiet except for plows on sidewalks and main streets. He had seen the cheerleader twice but she was always too far away. He was still unsure what he would do if they met, and he hadn't gotten her name.

If you asked what he remembered best he'd probably say the Friday before Christmas. That afternoon, Clear sat on the counting table next to the conveyor. He talked about the Bandstand that night and called it the biggest dance of the year. He mentioned Sara's and the blizzard forecast off the lake and told Lockett he'd pick him up early before most of it hit. For Lockett, Sara's bar was about becoming normal and getting loose and confident from two or three beers before the dance.

Around seven, they drove south in a light snow, past old barns and out buildings. Twenty minutes later, Clear pulled off the county road at the first intersection.

Behind the bar, a sharp-eyed Sara wore the dark red lipstick and the purple blouse she had on during the summer. Groups of juniors and seniors milled around with Hamm's and Budweiser. Sara's pudgy faced husband sat at the four stool bar next to two old farmers in blue bib overalls drinking Pabst. She punched open two Budweiser's and slid them toward Clear. She liked him. He never got drunk. He never caused trouble. And he knew how to laugh. Most importantly, he never ran off the road and brought the sheriff to her bar. She trusted him enough that she never checked Lockett's age. Fitz said Clear was the son she never had.

The blizzard started ninety minutes later. Clear drove cautiously without talking. He parked in an alley and they walked the cold half block to the VFW lobby. He told

Lockett he needed to piss and handed him his jacket and boots.

"Meet you upstairs."

The old veteran checker showed anchor tattoos with the letters USN on his wrists. He growled at two more snow covered coats but he shook the snow and hung them carefully.

Fresh balsam wreaths decorated oak bannisters and walls that curved ninety degrees to the second floor. Upstairs, Sinatra began, "Young at Heart."

Lockett climbed ten steps thinking about closing in on Christmas with half his shopping left. He looked up. The cheerleader came toward him. She glanced and passed. It was only a glance but he felt it in his legs. He blushed. Can you blush from being happy? She stopped a step below him. His first thought was a Thomas Hardy line: "I looked up from my writing and said what are you doing here?"

Her voice was alive.

"I know who you are."

His heart pounded. He thought about funny punch lines and how clever he was after two or three beers. He managed the words as he stepped down, across from her.

"I think we're neighbors."

She tossed her head, chin high, chest out, shoulders back. Sinatra's words mocked his nerves: "Fairy tales can come true, it can happen to you..."

Her eyes telegraphed energy before she spoke. Her mouth was wider.

"My name is Missy DuHarte," she said. "Molly is my real name. My grandmother's name was Molly. We moved here two years ago from Winnetka. I live across

34

the street from Patty Burke. Oliver, right? You went to school in Milwaukee. And sometimes you walk ahead of me."

She covered her mouth to hide a smile that went almost to grey green eyes, as if to say, "I saw you and you didn't see me."

The scent of balsam got heavier. Lockett opened his mouth to say something about their game of peekaboo. He hesitated.

Missy? No wonder Clear didn't mention her name. When does a Missy get her real name back?

They settled on opposite bannisters and began talking about whatever comes after a surprise. It wasn't the frivolous talk he imagined with a Missy, not like talking to a rich pampered girl with new clothes, a little white dog, symphony music, and a big house.

Sometimes, talking to a stranger was more exciting than to someone he knew, like talking to the new priest in the confessional. Those were the conversations that let him know things he didn't imagine. He didn't say, "You're beautiful," but that's what he thought.

She looked down after a group of girls passed.

"If we stay here we're going to create a lot of gossip."

He wasn't sure why, but he wanted to hear more from the voice with a hint of the south in it. He told her what Clear said.

"He makes girls feel safe," she said, "like an alpha wolf. They know he listens and protects. But we could never date."

Indian's and Missy's. That's why Clear didn't ask her out.

Lockett crossed his arms and changed the subject. He asked what surprised her most after she moved.

"It's so simple here," she said. "I love the library and the parks and the museum. I've got good teachers. But it's not very exciting. It's not home. It's not foreign. It's just space. My English teacher says we all need a sense of place. I go from half dreamy to nightmares. Someday, I want to travel. Places like Rome, Bali. Sometimes I think I'm in a kind of holding pen."

She leaned toward him.

"You're back. Does it feel like home? Do you think it's possible to be seduced by a place?"

His mind raced. Is she clever? Was she teasing?

"I like Jack London and Hemingway," he said, "I want to go to places like that."

He put his hands behind his back and gripped the banister. He told her an idea about two kites on the same string. She smiled at what he thought most girls would find weird.

"If they break loose," she said, "where do they end up?"

Lockett thought for a few seconds.

"What if they end up together," he said, "maybe Rome? The thing about good kites is that they do what they're made to do. People get seduced in Rome."

She grinned. The beer was working.

Lockett swallowed a smile. The conversation picked up, as if they needed to talk all night so everything got known all at once. He asked if she had a favorite book. She told him about a poet he didn't know. She said reading her was a way to survive when things were messy, "to keep windows open."

She talked about advanced English.

"It's Keats right now. My dad says if I feel like calling the author up, that's the test of quality. I would like to call Keats. Our teacher says if you follow the Nightingale you miss things. He says you're able to start at a deeper level if you read with someone else. I like that. I've asked Bobby but…"

She hesitated.

Lockett told her about Father Coyle who said to read Keats out loud and called it an experience. They had used two periods to talk about whether the world would be better if Keats had lived longer. The final exam had been one question: "Are revisions in life always better?"

They agreed about Ode to Autumn, about losses before winter. Coyle had said Keats was only five foot one and called the poem too feminine and sexual. But the idea of autumn and death had stuck.

"It sounds like you really wanted to be there, do you miss the teachers?"

He was sure some answer fit. Maybe one day he'd talk about it, but not right now, at least not the part that never seemed to go away. He told her everything depended on how they handled it.

"If you weren't ready, you didn't last. The place turned out different than I expected."

"Do you still believe in God that way? Would you ever go back?"

It was the wrong time. Lockett ducked the question.

He asked about her accent. She raised her arms to cover her ears. He blinked at the way her sweater showed her figure.

"My mother grew up in southern Missouri," she said. "They met in Rome when she was studying Italian. My dad called her *le Bella Figura*. She corrected him and said it was about decorum and manners much more than appearance. He liked that she wasn't shy. I hear it in my voice once in a while."

Her eyes sparkled. She fanned herself, like Scarlett O'Hara pretending to faint.

Lockett heard a small cough and looked up. Foley's face was red.

"What's going on? You two know each other?"

The question sounded confused, as if he meant to say how do you know each other. He coughed again, like working through something stuck in his throat. Lockett pictured him upstairs, checking his watch. He could almost hear his Milwaukee classmates chuckle at the long northern Wisconsin vowels, dooo, yooo, tooo, nooo. "Simpleton talk" they'd called it, "Grand Lac simp talk."

"We do now," Lockett said.

Foley hadn't expected that.

He pushed his hair out of his face and spread his feet. He leaned in, not quite sure, like a "B" movie star, and not doing it well. His voice was nervous.

"What the hell does that mean? Who the hell you think you are?"

More long vowels.

Lockett supposed he could rub it in, the seventh and eighth grade boxing lessons when the frustrated coach told Foley and two or three others, "Slide that left foot. Slide and jab. I can teach you to box if you care enough, but the key to fighting is that you don't care. That's how

38

you fight. If you care, you'll always be in trouble. Once you start hitting the guy, you never let up."

That was the year he walked to the Holy Rosary gym with his father for his first fight. He loved his father. He wanted his father to love him. Some of his friends had killed their first deer with their fathers. Others had committed to hard work with their fathers toward their Eagle Scout badge. This was his rite of passage. He wanted to do well.

For three rounds, his father sat ringside with a disgusted look. "Throw the right," he called, "throw the right." At the end, the referee raised the smiling eighth grader's hand. Outside the dressing room, his father scowled.

"You're twelve, start acting it. Tell your mother I had things to do at the bar."

Lockett froze at the silent message: "If you don't win you will betray or be betrayed."

Tears came during a long walk home in the heavy snow, angry at being cautious, ashamed at losing the fight. He wasn't who his father wanted him to be.

But tonight he was the intruder and enjoying it. Foley was overmatched in more ways than one, and making a fool of himself.

"We just met," Lockett said, "relax."

On the dance floor, Louis Armstrong began, "As Time Goes By." Molly grabbed Foley's arm. Her eyes broadcast what could have sounded silly.

"Listen Bobby, a kiss is just a kiss. Good music should make us closer."

The idea sounded sincere from someone who made sense and wasn't shy about it. Foley missed what she said as though waiting for something after, "We do now."

Foley was still searching for the answer when he grabbed her wrist. She turned. Her knuckles brushed Lockett's hip. Foley never broke stride. He was still talking when he let her go at the bottom step. She turned and waved with four fingers, like Gregorian chant that touched and moved away.

Lockett was thrilled. Whatever Foley was talking about wouldn't matter. By the time they said good night, Lockett would be like someone laying flowers on Foley's grave.

The beer was still working. He cupped his hands and called: "I'll read to you."

She waved again. Her smile stayed with him, as good as a kiss. He took the rest of the steps two at a time.

He watched Clear tease a pretty black-haired girl with jitterbug pivots as if they had been there before. The Bill Haley record ended. Clear spotted him and said something to the girl who nodded and smiled.

He grinned.

"Foley couldn't find her, really pissed. Can you imagine anyone sweeter? Did you ask her out?"

Lockett was overjoyed at the idea that made him smile. "Not yet."

He shrugged. "I think I'll walk home, see you tomorrow."

He walked a few steps and turned. Clear was still looking.

"Go ahead, freeze your ass off."

Lockett grinned and cocked his head, "I think I'm in the movies. You gonna take her home?"

Clear inhaled.

"You got a better chance of seeing God in the next thirty minutes. If you can't have fun with her, you belong in Milwaukee. You may not get another chance."

He poked his tongue in his cheek to keep from laughing.

"Yeh. Never underestimate pretty."

Lockett turned and smiled. It might be twenty degrees but he'd be warm with his thoughts about the steps.

Slanting snow blew drifts on top of two feet already in most places. He crunched through it like in kindergarten where he colored it grey and worried Miss French would scold him again for not making it white.

Colored crayons and kindergarten, all he had to do was show up. But Molly would be a challenge, and this time he wouldn't be cautious.

He followed ruts made by a big truck down Tower avenue. Fresh footprints led in and out of three bars. Snowed blurred the Budweiser sign pink on the one his father had owned. Inside all three, customers talked about the weather like the third person in conversations that mixed manhood myths with joking and learning when to push back. Alcohol was a badge of fuck- it -all courage, almost as important as anti-freeze, and more important for the nightly drama's about who would win. Until each winter when somebody's heart gave out shoveling snow in his driveway and people stepped back long enough to say he should have known better at his age, shoveling, drunk. They also said, if you want to be lonely, get sober in Grand Lac.

Three blocks later, the ruts turned east through more drifts. Wind that had blown from behind poured west down Belknap with sounds Lucque would have enjoyed. Maybe that's why the blind priest entered the sanctuary for Mass refusing to be different, straightening his vestments, smiling as if he could see, and giving the best sermons.

"Once I thought I had to go out and meet things," he said, "because I was blind. But I found out that they came to me instead. I never had to go more than halfway and the world would be friendly to what I wanted. Do what you can with what you have. Find the innocence in other people. See what happens."

Lockett smiled at times like tonight when Lucque would have asked: "*Vis vitae*, a new life force? It's not anybody's job to make us feel better. A relationship should let us see what we feel, and what might change. Love yourself so you know how to love others. What do you see? What do you think? Why have a brain if you're not curious?"

He turned south on Hammond. Wind gusts carried cracking sounds from a switch engine in the Soo Line yards. Large Christmas trees showed lights in windows like traditional cards that never got old.

He passed big homes for seven blocks until he stopped a block over on Cummings. A street light made shadows on the branches of a thirty foot spruce next to Patty Burke's house. He strained to see the dark second story windows on the house he had walked past dozens of times. She was home now, in warm pajamas, the curves of her body shifting, a few inches here, a few inches there.

42

The priests would have lectured him: "Weary virtue, desire eaten away by appetite, a man walking to nowhere with his disgraceful sin."

The outline of a large car disappeared around the corner on Hammond. Lockett listened to the sound of his boots in the snow as he walked to his house. In a few minutes, he would trade one storm for another. It was two blocks from Molly's, but everything felt more like two hundred miles.

His father had come of age during the height of myths about the great American male. He represented a time that rewarded ambition by men who worked hard, made money, and never thought it would end. He wore expensive double-breasted suits with new ties and made sure his family traveled on first class trains with sleeper suites.

All that was gone. His failure was losing the bar. Before that, he brought home cash that marked success. When the money stopped, so did he. He never admitted anything. He never asked for help. Twice he painted houses and drank the money away. The family was hiding what they thought were secrets about alcohol and getting poor. In some ways, he and his father shared failures as prisoners of old worlds.

The storm began at Lockett's bedroom door.

"What have you been up to? You keep your mother worried wandering around in this weather."

Most of what his father said had stopped mattering. But for Lockett, the idea of home included a notion of being important enough to be accepted or at least to come and go. Tonight he would remember, "Won't you ever get it right?" He promised himself that, like his temporary tracks in the snow, one day he would leave it behind.

Sometimes he thought Clear wasn't the only one without a father.

He sat at his back window and watched snow cover the ledge. He listened to plows pushing drifts over curbs toward her house. He smiled at the unexpected kiss from her knuckles and the new friendship that the priests would have forbidden. His shoulders got tight when he thought about moving past her on the steps, smiling, or barely slowing.

Twenty minutes later, he closed his eyes. There had been no epiphany. But there had been a special connection. The experiences with the priests and the meeting on the steps were what Joyce had called a "memorable phase."

He imagined waking from a dream to a pretty girl who represented everything he ever imagined, in a boring city where they didn't fit. She was beautiful and confident and smart. And she didn't pretend she wasn't. He may not be necessary for Molly Duharte, but he could love her and be loved.

He thought about the conversation again, what she said about Foley not reading with her. He fell asleep smiling about kites. Something unusual was happening.

THE LIGHT WE LEAVE BEHIND

*"At least I know who I was when I got up
this morning but I think I must have changed
several times since then."*

Lewis Carroll, *Alice in Wonderland*

Molly never left his mind on Saturday. He glanced at the clock at least twice every hour. In between he replayed the dance. At work, Clear kidded him about his walk in the storm and talked about the Danielson twin he took home in his warm car. After supper, Lockett made the call.

"Could I speak to Molly, please?"

A few seconds later, something inside vibrated. They tied up the phone for two hours with ideas they hadn't finished on the VFW steps. Her laugh opened something else. He called her twice the next week.

By Christmas Eve, he had almost daydreamed his way to Guenard's candy shop. A few minutes before it closed, the owner's young wife added a green bow to a red box of truffles. He watched the sun set and felt the temperature drop at Molly's back door. She thanked him.

"I'll think of it when I look at the stars on my way to church," she said. "I know it's only their light, but we're all like the stars. We leave light behind, especially when people die."

She grinned and clapped her hands.

"Chocolate peanut butter cups and now truffles. Maybe I'm decadent!"

She told him she was reading poetry by Rossetti, the author he didn't recognize on the stairs.

45

"Her poems can make you know what you didn't know you knew."

She laughed. "Did I just say that?"

She pointed to a page near the beginning of the green book and asked him to read. She closed her eyes as if hearing something behind the words.

> "Thus two of three took death for love and won
> him after strife;
> One droned on in sweetness like a fatted bee:
> All on the threshold, yet all short of life."

"Thank you. It's not as simple as it seems. I hope I don't die fat or sad."

Lockett was struck by the poem's idea that a death could be an opportunity to see a whole life.

She squeezed his free hand.

"It's your gift. I apologize for not wrapping it. Merry Christmas."

She hesitated.

"There's something you should know."

She paused again.

"It hasn't been going well with Bobby for a long time. There are some good things but he's not reliable. He doesn't know me. He doesn't remember my birthday. He doesn't know my classes. That's all important. I've been pretending. It makes me feel sad. His friends know it, my friends know it, it's never about us. My dad says if you look at the pain you cause as the other person's fault, that's evil. Sometimes Bobby does that. I think of what I've been missing."

She paused again, this time for a long time.

"Our parents play bridge together. That's how we started dating. I have to decide what comes next."

She moved close. She surprised him with a long hug. The kiss on his cheek was more than just something nice.

There was another short pause.

"You can trust me," she said.

The real cold hit around ten. An hour later, Lockett walked to the Holy Rosary Cathedral knowing bright stars and a clear night meant it would get colder.

He had served the Midnight Mass for six years. The pageantry still appealed. But serving had become like a line from *Portrait of an Artist:* "When you wet the bed, first it gets warm and then it gets cold." This would be his last year as an altar boy.

The sacristy filled with juniors and seniors jockeying for one of the half dozen new cotton cassocks. Somewhere he had read, "The minute you settle for less than you deserve, you get even less than you settle for." It had been on his mind when he wrote the letter, and now with the cassock. Later he would do more than just jockey with Foley.

An old nun took roll and gave instructions: "Walk slowly, focus on a pew's distance between yourself and the person in front of you."

The cotton cassock felt almost cool on his shoulders. But somewhere, not far below the surface of the nun's words, was a warning about the guy behind him in a heavy wool cassock who got overheated and sick and vomited on his neck.

Lucque would have called the scent of whiskey and the slurred words from priests "palatable mediocrity." What did they hope for? What were their fears? What chance did they have now, middle aged or old, upside down with alcohol or other secrets in ways most people never imagined?

At midnight, the organ opened with the Hallelujah Chorus. Father Theodosius Barrens led the procession carrying a six- foot gold cross like a Druid magician celebrating with a wand. Sixteen altar boys and forty priests followed two by two, ahead of the bishop.

The name Theodosius came from a disgraced pope who claimed that Jesus was God and died early from wine and "excesses of the flesh." Holy Rosary parishioners whispered Barren's pinkie ring might be hiding something.

What Lockett knew best happened three years earlier. His mother had just returned from Saturday confessions. She stood looking out the kitchen window. She turned with tears in her eyes.

"He told me I should be ashamed for asking about birth control," she said.

Later, Barrens' was convicted for his own excesses of the flesh as one of the diocese' first priest predators.

Thirty minutes later, Lockett listened to the bishop's almost casual sermon, nothing about wise men, shepherds or swaddling clothes.

"Jesus command is to revolutionize this life," he said. "If you don't, your eternal life may be at risk. He is asking us to put our faith in something we know we can trust. Today is a day to do just that with him, to celebrate all that you have and all that you might have."

Lockett closed his eyes. The spot on his cheek where she kissed him tingled like it had been frozen. The more he rubbed it, the better it felt. The scent of balsam drifted from trees on the altar, the same scent as the wreaths on the VFW walls. He imagined her Presbyterian church two blocks away and a sanctuary filled with blue spruce and white lights. Maybe she listened to "Hark the Herald Angels Sing." Maybe she heard a short sermon about peace and joy, or something Lucque might say: "Find a place inside you where there is joy, and the joy will burn out the pain."

The congregation would end with "Silent Night," and shake hands and say Merry Christmas. Families would leave for gifts and food and affection and sleep. Maybe next year he would be with her. Maybe that was an answer to what they had both been missing.

At three o'clock, the Cathedral doors opened and everything changed. Cold air drifted up all three aisles. Tired classmates sang "Angels We Have Heard On High" with cheerfulness like the season. Parishioners disappeared into the below zero night as if they hardly knew each other.

The old nun drummed her fingers on the counter as she watched the boys hang their cassocks. Lockett hung his with a sense of relief. But he reached and touched it with both hands one last time.

As they left the church, Mousey Dunn shuffled behind with a deformed leg. The church and school had become the pious janitor's home, early in the morning to late in the evening, away from the neighborhood near the tracks where kids plugged cardboard inside shoes to cover holes in the bottoms.

"Merry Christmas, Oliver," he said.

"Thank you, Mr. Dunn, Merry Christmas."

"Let us hope," Mousey said.

He touched Lockett's arm.

"Life is not gentle, Oliver, but God is good. Keep a good heart."

A minute later, the air felt thinner. The wind off the lake made it easy to hurry. Colored lights flickered across front lawns with dark patches under evergreens. Maybe the bishop was right. Maybe this was the time to celebrate all that we had or might have. Somehow, Mousey didn't seem alone.

Almost three weeks passed. Lockett worked through different messages for Foley almost every day. When the time came, he would know what to say. No Macbeth, no condolences, Foley could never trade up. He would be pissed.

Nobody had seen the sun for a week when finals began in January. The first afternoon, senior football players sat at a long table in the far corner of the crowded library. Foley and McIntyre sat next to each other whispering with their backs to the door. Three players on the other side grinned as Lockett walked toward their table. Foley turned. Lockett said it loud enough for the table to hear.

"Call it divine intervention, Bobby. She's my girl now."

Someone scraped his feet. Someone else laughed. McIntyre threw his hands in the air and laughed the loudest. Foley stood half way. He hesitated, like listening to water when it hit the drain. McIntyre pulled him back into his chair. Foley sat, like he realized he had the math wrong again.

Sister Julian looked up from her desk in the middle of the room. She put down the book she was reading. She stared, as if she wasn't surprised by anything junior and senior boys did. She stood and crossed her arms and moved toward the table. Her eyes narrowed at Lockett.

"You, sit down, over there, or leave."

Lockett sat down. A few minutes later, the seniors walked out. McIntyre threw his arm around Foley's neck, still laughing, as if flowers on his grave were funny.

January and February were just alike in 1955. Days started with icy cold mornings. Nights were the same.

None of that mattered when they threw their skates over their shoulders and walked to the shack next to the rink where a man named Ted fed wood into a pot-bellied stove. He smiled when he tightened a girl's skates and stuttered when he talked, but he succeeded with "thank you" each time Molly gave him a dime.

For the rest of the winter, Lockett got excited by simple things each time they skated. Some nights, she slipped her hand deep into his jacket pocket. Some nights, she leaned against his shoulder and they didn't talk for a full circle around the rink. They laughed when he held her forearms and guided her down between his legs until she touched the ice. He couldn't remember laughing that hard with anybody.

"I watched you at Nebagamon," she said. "Bobby said you went to school in Milwaukee. You seemed very shy. Other people actually said that to me, that you were shy. I thought you were interesting. My dad says that should be a criteria. I remember my mind scrambling the first time I saw you on the way to school. The air smelled so fresh."

He hadn't thought about it before, listening that close to someone trying to answer questions about him that he hadn't answered himself.

Before Valentine's Day, Lockett sensed a new direction for old energy. He stopped cutting classes and catching up. He put ten dollars down on a portable record player from the music store on Tower avenue and agreed to pay the rest in thirty days. The owner called it "the best little portable" he had seen.

Valentine's Day she grabbed the sides of her head and grinned before she threw her arms around him.

"I can't believe this."

Later she told him her father guessed it must have cost two pay checks.

Like every year, winter needed more patience. Spring hinted then backed off. Locals said this was the longest winter, but they said that every year. Skating finished. Molly gave Ted a silver dollar and big hug. His eyes lit up like they were both firsts.

On Friday's, Lockett skipped the last period study hall and walked the block to Central's pep rally. Standing in the gym doorway told everyone that Molly Duharte was getting serious with a new guy from Holy Rosary. Later she told him, "When you know someone special, seeing them look at you can be hard. I get so nervous, Oliver's here, don't look at me. But I'm happy you're there."

After the games, they joined the crowd at the restaurant across from the courthouse with jukebox lyrics for teenage instincts.

"I get so lonely I could die."

She told him about Gershwin who encouraged young composers to see American music as important, and

Glenn Miller who shifted music away from jazz, and The Four Freshmen who set the standard for harmony. She mentioned her favorite song, "Not a Day Goes By" from an old musical called *Merrily We Roll Along*.

"Songs aren't necessarily about us," she said, "but that one takes something sad and turns it into something beautiful, how much someone cared."

She took a deep breath.

"I like that," she said, "what happens after the words run out. It says no good thing ever dies. I think that's how it is."

He had heard the song. The pain of regretting and caring so much at the same time seemed complete. It might depend. But on what? He knew she was right about whatever it meant.

Two brown hooded missionaries arrived from St. Louis for the "retreat" in late March. The first morning, junior and senior boys filed to the church past melting snow that smelled like decaying winter.

Father Blake pulled his glasses down and looked over the wire rims. The only pink on his face came from two ears that hung like wings. His voice was full.

"It is primitive behavior and you must struggle toward God in purity and silence, beating down the devil who builds his power through that little girl. And you may find yourself in the middle of conflict and contradiction between yourself and her because your ability to tell what is real and what is false has succumbed to passion. But you will not please God with those contradictions. Don't you agree, Father Spain?"

Spain was thick, like he lifted weights. As if on cue, he said, "Yes Father, I do."

He began in a soft voice with a warning: "To be a virtuous man you must resist her like your worst enemy as she manipulates to create whatever she wants. And you will have feelings of infinite desire so intense that you will gasp. But if you are virtuous, you will know that they are treacheries from Satan, resurrected again and again from hell. And you will find a sack full of reasons to allow that little girl to push her tongue between your lips like Satan's snake, to ignore the flames of hell, just that one time, to touch her in places that God has set aside for marriage."

"If you masturbate, or even touch yourself, your fingers will rot off like a leper's. And if you touch that little girl's breast, your hands will burn the hottest of any place on your body."

By the time he finished, he was pounding his fist in his hand and sweating. Classmates fidgeted and looked at each other. Some cleared their throats. Maybe it wasn't on purpose, but Spain's words scared everyone enough to keep them frozen in their seats, even if they wet their pants like Jake Kurowski.

The day had begun with another message about superstition and guilt from adult men scaring boys about girls. That afternoon, the girls walked to the church. Lockett assumed the new villain was "that little boy."

When the girls returned, the nuns introduced lengths of butcher's twine knotted every half inch and measured to fit around waists.

"Finger the chastity belts like the rosary during temptations," they said. "Buy one to remain pure and God will reward you with a pure husband or wife. The cost is fifty cents."

The women who dressed in black and told their secrets to men like Blake and Spain in dark boxes had bought into another tricky missionary idea.

That night, he told Molly about the missionaries. She clapped and laughed. She quoted Keats, "the strenuous tongue that could burst a grape." She moved behind the kitchen table and clamped her hands between her legs. She was serious and funny and she knew it.

"We bring our tongues to worship, not just in church. And the snake isn't a real snake you know."

Later, they looked back and saw Blake and Spain as she had seen Ahab, "Strange virtues, people so obsessed going after one thing that they lose sight of everything else."

About this time, the weather changed. Walking replaced skating. Snow melted and exposed the usual winter debris: lost mittens, silver beer cans, a dead bird, a used Kotex. Christmas tricycles appeared. People lined up at gas stations to pump air into tires on bicycles stored since October. Lake ice melted nearly two weeks early. A seventy degree day brought a confused bee, an early crocus, and Perez Prado's "Cherry Pink and Apple Blossom White." Lockett cringed each time he knew the driver who honked and drove by in a new Packard or an old DeSoto.

Summer passed quickly. A week before Christmas, the music store owner suggested *In the We Small Hours of the Morning,* with a photo on the cover of Sinatra standing in an empty street.

"Best album of the year," the owner said, "perfect with the record player."

He wrapped it in gold paper with red ribbon and added a green felt poinsettia.

Christmas Eve, Molly's green wool sheath showed her figure. Red mittens and a black and red cashmere scarf matched her red coat with black buttons. Lockett blinked and stared. Instinct, he thought, you can't teach stuff like that. He reached out and touched her shoulders.

"You look amazing," he said, "gorgeous."

She stepped back and grinned.

"My mother says someone isn't born a woman, she becomes one."

Snow fell on their walk to church like the lyrics from "White Christmas."

The usher at the church entrance stammered.

"Merry Christmas, Missy. Nice to see you Oliver."

A year earlier, Andy Gault had married and switched from Holy Rosary to Hammond Avenue Presbyterian. They talked briefly about the two years when Gault coached the American Legion baseball team. Gault reached for Molly's hand, trying to relax. "You look very pretty," he said, still excited about two Catholics at a Presbyterian church on Christmas Eve.

Minutes later, the minister began his sermon about the gift of the Magi. He called it "the wise gift, the kind of gift that makes you rich, the gift of ourselves."

The choir ended with "Go Tell It On The Mountain." As they left, Gault whispered, "You're lucky." Lockett remembered the bishop's sermon, a time to celebrate.

Molly covered her mouth as she opened the album next to the seven-foot spruce in her living room. She had obviously guessed. But she leaned over and they hugged. She pulled a small box wrapped in craft paper and raffia from under the tree.

The Parker 51 pen had been engraved on the gold barrel, O.A.L.

"My parents gave me one for eighth grade graduation," she said. "I still have it. You want what's important in your life to be enjoyed by others."

She folded her hands on her lap.

"Sometimes I think God is a metaphor for something bigger than ourselves. We're not that different, Oliver. We believe in the same God. I'm glad we're together tonight."

She cleared her throat. Her voice was shaky.

"Would you ever go back?"

It was hard for Lockett to tell how surprised he was. He had told her some things, about the book report, the rector, and the priest who asked what his father did. She knew his questions about religion. This was the second time she asked about the story that still pulled at him. She had become more than a friend he could let in to his secrets. He needed her for this.

"The past is our definition," Lucque had said, "we escape it only by doing something better."

"Well," he said, "in the beginning, everything opened up. I thought I could be a priest, I thought God wanted that. I thought I could and I thought I should, then everything shut down. Things happened, things I thought were firm were gone. I learned that maybe God hadn't meant it, but he never said what he wanted. He didn't say anything and I didn't say anything and that's about where it ended. I thought he was finished trying."

He talked about the Saturday during the short Thanksgiving vacation with the farm boys from Minnesota who stayed behind.

"It was just too far for us to go home," he said, "Grand Lac, St. Cloud."

He told her about Father Fagan who taught philosophy and Latin, how he led the prayer and chatted while players showered and dressed after every game.

It started when Fagan offered to help with irregular plural nouns in Latin.

"I remember the rain on the windows in the apartment, like saying thanks for the chance to meet alone. I thought we were finished when he leaned over and put his hand on my knee. He began talking grades. He moved his hand higher and asked about different sounds I heard at night. He asked me to make one of the noises.

I wasn't sure which noise he meant. The rules said no talking after ten when the lights went out in the dorms. I guessed he meant sounds from dreams in the middle of the night, or the fast breathing. When I didn't answer, he smiled and squeezed my thigh. He asked if I knew what people did when they had sex. He said he knew I didn't have a foreskin. I jerked his hand away when he moved it higher. He rubbed himself. Something different happened. He moaned and grunted. I told him I had to go. He stayed quiet until I got to the door. He smiled like it was all a joke. He said *res ipsa loquitur*. It means the thing speaks for itself. He said there were certain kinds of privacy that didn't have to be explained to anyone. He told me to remember that no one had seen us together."

Lockett said he was sure what happened was wrong. But the school frowned on weakness from students. Complaining was for weaker men. Future priests were expected to figure things out. But Christ had said, "Father forgive them," not "Everything is fine." He thought about telling Lucque. Maybe God had chosen him for this kind of challenge.

"At some point, I realized what was happening. I was in the wrong place."

Lockett finished. He had talked for twenty minutes. Explaining a foreskin could be complicated.

"No," he said, "I won't go back."

She almost whispered, "The most precious gift we can offer is the gift of ourselves." Tears filled her eyes. "It's a lot more emotional than I thought. Thank you."

She smiled.

"Yes, I know what a foreskin is."

Lockett wondered if he could convert like Gault.

Spring scheduled itself in 1956 like an apology for winter like it did every year. Lake ice shrunk fifty percent in March. Wives aired moth ball smells from stored clothes and hung wool underwear on new clothes lines.

Molly's kitchen served for homework together at least one night a week. For thirty minutes, English or history became an introduction to the real purpose of the evening. They laughed at something, touched, then got quiet. Sometimes, after their tongues touched, they laughed

59

again. More than once her mother pushed through the swinging kitchen door and saw Molly on his lap.

"Missy," she said, enough to end whatever they were doing.

Le bella figura.

Prom week was announced in time for dates and dresses. They had skipped his prom in 1955, after the principal warned about low necklines, exposed skin, and dates from other schools. She had already told Gilbert Downs that he couldn't attend in '56 because of his Mohawk haircut. A few days later, Steve Huber suggested double dating for the prom instead of the restaurant across the bay as they had planned. He wanted to show off his new girlfriend.

"They won't stop our dates," he said. "Hell, a smart Protestant and a smart Jew? Both cheerleaders? They'll fit. A lot of guys are gonna be jealous."

Down's experience meant things hadn't gotten any better. But Molly's eyes sparkled when Lockett explained the idea.

"Do you think it's alright?" she said.

"To be honest, no, but we'll be OK."

He was still not sure about dates from other schools on prom night when Holy Rosary cheerleaders chatted with both girls on the convent steps before the nun's inspection.

Molly's cheek bones looked more defined since Christmas. Her swept back hair made her look older. She had shopped in Minneapolis with her mother and found a strapless pink dress with the right fit. Huber's dark-haired date stood out in a backless yellow dress with a full skirt.

Lockett watched other male appetites sneak looks. It may have been pride or he may have been too protective, but he was the only one who could touch Molly Duharte.

Mary Dunphy and her date joined them in the greeting line. Mary was the best student in the senior class, the most mature, and the captain of the cheerleaders whose family wealth had practically built the church in 1927. When they reached the convent door, Sister Serena stared at Mary's tight, red low cut dress. Mary returned the stare.

"Sisters, let me introduce our guests," she said. "Estelle Bloom is Steve's date. She's goes to Duluth East. She's in the senior choir with a scholarship to Brandeis next year. Her father is a doctor. Molly Duharte is a student at Central. She's a junior. She's on the honor roll. She's also a cheerleader. Her father is head of the chemistry department at the college."

Sister Serena was cool and restrained.

"It's a pleasure to meet each of you."

Introductions to the other nun's lasted a minute before Serena seemed to relax. She asked a young nun to show all three couples to the convent parlor, she would join them in a few minutes.

Huber had been right.

Later Mary said, "God doesn't get excited about a bra."

Molly grinned.

"At least Sister knows I'm not a pagan. My dad says we could be Catholic, at least around the edges. He may not be kidding."

Lockett looked at the ground.

The music sounded like more than about dancing: Dean Martin's "Memories Are Made of This," Vic Damone's "On the Street Where You Live," the McGuire Sisters, "Picnic."

"We've all seen the devil," she said, "don't you think? If we were to make love, it's about the bottoms of my feet. It goes up my legs."

Her voice faded.

"If you don't like being seduced..."

Lockett crossed his arms. What he said next sounded anxious and absurd and he knew it.

"It's about discipline," he said. "Irish Catholics sleep head to toe. That might work."

"You make me laugh," she said. "That and cold showers? Is that another way they taught you to stay celibate? And you think it will work for us? It's about appetite. It's not always about babies."

Lockett thought about the prayer by St. Thomas More: "God, give me a sense of humor. But give me someone to share it with."

They had never talked about getting pregnant, like they never talked about being apart. But every now and then, he thought about marriage and college, and a part time job. Tonight would come before anything else.

A little after midnight, they walked the curved beach along the lake carrying the red and black checkered blanket he had used at St. Ignatius. They listened to small waves near the mouth of Dutchman's Creek, where Clear's father had wanted to return, where the Ojibwa had a burial ground, a mile away. The area above the beach was well drained with tall grasses. Minutes later they reached a grove in the middle of birch trees. The blanket would serve another purpose tonight.

She cradled his face with her hands.

"I dreamed of this with you," she said.

He stroked her feet.

"Is it alright?"

That was his last fumbling thought. Twenty seconds later he lost control and warm ejaculate covered her stomach. He heard himself breathing, as close to crying as he could get. He trapped the sounds in his throat. Throwing her into a risk with pregnancy should have been gentle and giving. Frustration, desire and shame all came with his tears.

She took his hands.

"Please Oliver, sex is more than performing. What if I told you my body gets moist just being around you? Sometimes it happens. I'm here, I'm glad."

They used their handkerchiefs and the edges of the blanket to clean up. They laid on the slope and watched an early summer moon until they fell asleep in each other's arms.

The sun rose a few hours later with the scent of new grass. Light on the horizon showed blue water as far as they could see. Molly tilted her head at an early robin chirping.

She smiled.

"He knows something special happened here."

They talked about robins who mate and migrate, and the special happiness they must feel coming back to where they were born.

"Take my hands, Oliver, touch me here and here. Imagine eating warm raspberry's, early in the morning."

This time he knew, putting her in his mouth, learning corrections the way a child learns different spaces with its tongue. Maybe God was a flavor.

"Wider," he said.

That summer, buds blossomed earlier and more often. Bees and butterflies pollinated and everybody took them for granted. Like Candide, nothing bad could happen in this, the best of all worlds.

It was impossible to imagine they would go beyond the lake without each other.

FALL OUT

"Our moods do not believe in each other."

Ralph Waldo Emerson, *Circles*

In June, Lockett was sure of three things: Molly was his best friend, he needed a car, and the draft was out there somewhere. When anyone asked him about his plans after graduation he could only say he didn't know. Worse yet, everything had wasted away with his father. Coming home at night seemed more like breaking and entering.

His uncle Hugh had offered a job on the railroad as a clerk. The money was good, Lockett could work hours that allowed him to go to school, and a career like Hugh's seemed possible. Hugh knew his brother would think of the idea as charity.

"Ask your father, the job's yours," Hugh said.

His father exploded.

"No son of mine is going to work the railroads. The railroads are dead. I'll have a talk with Hugh about this."

Lockett never learned about their conversation. Neither uncle Hugh or his father ever mentioned the idea again.

Lockett told Molly, "He doesn't get me, he doesn't particularly want to. The only thing we have in common is the last name."

In late June, a month after graduation, and six weeks after the prom, the discussion began like every talk since.

"Did you ever think about what her parents thought, keeping that young girl out all night?" His face turned red. "You won't ever amount to anything that way." He stepped back with his chin out. "You're not using the car any more, pulling a stunt like that, twice."

Lockett had seen it too many times.

"I'll get my own."

His father snapped.

"Not in this town. I'll see to that, not in this town. You're not bringing around another car while I'm explaining all the talk."

He paused.

"I want you out of here, find your own place you want to be a big shot."

Lockett walked away and turned.

"Fuck you. When you die, it's not going to be much different around here than it is right now."

He slammed the back door. He knew his words had said everything. Even when he was angry, his father never used "fuck." The part about dying was more than cruel.

Ten minutes later, he made his way past the post office. Flags hung straight down. He glanced at a row of recruiting signs. He walked another block and entered the newspaper from the alley. The wet day would be his first absence in two years. It was his eighteenth birthday, and the foreman agreed.

The pool hall in the next block was empty except for cigarette smoke and two old pros betting masse' shots on the large snooker table. For the next four hours, he forgot everything except the argument. He alternated between angry and sad. He thought of his father and his eyes, his and Spencer Tracy's. And the times he'd watched old Tracy movies, where Tracy died at the end. He remembered the plastic torches that lit both sides of the dark screen as he wiped tears from his face and waited as long as he could to leave the theater.

Around four thirty he drank a bottle of root beer and practiced eight ball for fifteen minutes. He waved to the old men and stepped into the cool lake wind that played with the city every summer.

He walked toward the post office going nowhere. Two years in the Marines might have been time enough to sort things out in a different world. What the hell, it had certainly worked out for Powers.

The tall Navy petty officer showed two rows of ribbons on his chest. He said the Marine recruiter had stepped out. Lockett cursed under his breath. It was almost five, the Marine probably wouldn't be back. The petty officer told him he could give him the same test the Marines gave. Five minutes later, he laid a plastic sheet over fifty multiple choice answers. He marked two or three places and smiled.

"Pretty good. I can give you any school you want. You learn a trade, get three squares a day and a warm bunk at night. Better than carrying around a seventy-five pound pack and sleeping in mud trenches. Can't give you a three year hitch at eighteen. But it's worth it for one more. Sign up now, you get the G.I. Bill when you get out. And you get to spend the rest of the summer here. You don't leave until October. How's that sound?"

Lockett didn't answer. He reached over and signed three papers.

He regretted it before he left the building. He'd become like too many he knew, fumbling around all their lives, listening to too much talk about leaving. How do you explain something that quick, before you're ready? What do you say to Molly?

He wandered until the coffee shop three miles away where he read newspapers and drank free fill ups. At ten, he surprised her at the dairy store where the manager insisted he employed only smart hard working girls to make strawberry sundaes and chocolate sodas and sell milk. If they happened to be pretty, he claimed he never noticed.

She leaned her head on his shoulder during the walk to her house. He smelled her hair. She looked up when he told her. She shook her head and turned to hide her tears. She sighed.

"What do you want me to do? In some ways, I know it's not a choice. I'll miss you."

She looked down and stopped.

"It's not that. It's not all about that. Even in my sleep you know me. I'm afraid you won't come back."

They walked another block. This time she pleaded.

"Can you understand being alone?"

Lockett caught himself holding his breath. She was right. She wasn't plain. She didn't have to be alone. She had given him her best. What responsible friend wouldn't want the best for her?

The saddest tears came at her back door. For the first time, he knew a teenage girl heaving sobs as her heart broke in two. He put his tongue on his teeth, as if there was nothing more to say. He should have talked to her. Maybe she would have accepted two years in the Marines. He had made a choice like he hated their happiness.

"I just want you to be happy," she said.

She wiped at her tears.

"Would you mind if I gave you your present later?"

Candide was over.

The next morning, his mother took a deep breath. Lockett had been too ashamed to bring Molly to his house and they had never been introduced. But his mother had smiled a few weeks earlier.

"I think I saw your friend with one of the Burke girls down the street. She's a pretty girl."

She asked if Molly knew. Lockett said yes.

"Oh," she said.

She wanted to believe what he told her about avoiding the draft and learning a skill. But her mother's love saw through the lie. Happiness drained from her face. She pressed her fist to her lips. She said it quickly.

"If that's what you want, for pity's sake, let's have no more talk of it."

A year later, he told her he had been transferred to his ship in Pearl Harbor. Memories of Grand Lac sailors who died in the Second World War came back. It hadn't been that long for her.

That summer seemed sunnier. His father changed his mind about the car. Drive-in movies and beaches added hours with Molly.

Otherwise nothing had changed. That's what he thought, or wanted to think. But the Navy decision had made it harder. They had come to a place where she suffered. It was easier when he imagined her like Foley or the priests, like objects he had chosen to end with. He couldn't say it was the Navy. He had chosen that too.

She had mentioned it only once.

On a bright July Saturday afternoon, they had walked to the park on the western edge of the lake. Molly had rolled the sleeves of the blue button down shirt and worn white shorts that emphasized her long legs. They ate cups of chocolate ice cream on a bench at the park pavilion and talked about what she was reading.

"I'll finish Thoreau before school starts," she said. She stopped and stared at her hands.

"He has a line that goes, 'Beware any activity that requires new clothes.'"

She bit the side of her cheek. There were tears in her eyes.

The first Sunday in September, Lockett said goodnight to her parents. He passed the library with hundreds of books, a glass top coffee table, a bowl of apples, drawings over the fireplace and a new black and white television. Her mother's grandparents had been original Missouri settlers who became wealthy from land and agriculture. Her father had left Northwestern for a simpler career in Grand Lac.

Lockett heard screams from the Ed Sullivan audience. The camera focused above Elvis' waist as he gyrated to "Don't be Cruel."

"What do you think of this fellow," her father asked. Lockett thought Presley and Chuck Berry and Little Richard were selling noise. He swallowed hard.

"I know he's popular," he said.

Her father leaned back in his chair and nodded.

A few minutes later, the cold wind stung Lockett's nose like smelling salts and revealed the wet spot on his jeans. The real questions registered: Can you think? What about emotional growth? What are those impulses that deliver pain to my daughter? He seemed to have missed the wet spot.

Lockett had hoped the night before he left would go without much more suffering. They agreed that tears at the depot would just add more sadness. His father would take him to the station.

They ate at the Pick Wick, where they had planned to go before the prom. He thought the expensive restaurant would be enjoyable and it was.

As they left, she took his hand.

"My period came early, Oliver."

It came as an apology. Her voice was sad and it was the sadness that hurt, not the words. The words could have meant anything. In a way he relaxed. Ideas about their last night together had become uncomfortable. Tonight, intimacy could have led to more ache. Better to say goodnight to her here without more tears tomorrow. There will be other nights.

He squeezed her hand.

"I'll be home for Christmas, that's only a couple of months."

She smiled. "I know. The next time I'll be ready."

He had wanted the evening to be pleasant. That's all he wanted. But he knew it was not without suffering. He still wasn't sure about his decision on October eighth. It was not something he wanted to think about walking through the St. Paul train station with a handful of wide eyed mid-west farm boys who had said goodbye to people they loved. He consoled himself with ideas about free board and room, a steady income, and money to send home at the end of every month. He told himself it would all be over before he knew it. And somewhere along the line, answers would come.

A very tall lieutenant led the induction oath while Vin Scully announced the only perfect game in World Series history from a radio in the next room.

"I will protect and defend…" "Larson checks the sign from Berra…"

Almost immediately, Lockett heard the seminary message designed to change young males from adolescents into warriors. "Wonderfully severe training in hardihood" someone had said.

Beyond that, he hurt to think he hadn't done things differently.

Two years later he had become more critical of himself, trying to balance what he had done, and it was costing him. Molly had sensed his feelings and begun to respond.

The turning point came when she broke the relationship. Her letter said she never meant to hurt him. Time by herself was hard, she said. "I miss you, I think of you all the time." She repeated what she said at Christmas: "You want what's important in your life to be shared by others. It's hard in a vacuum. I'm sorry."

Lockett worked to think of words to describe the monotony she must have felt in Grand Lac. She had suffered for two years, the time the Marine hitch would have lasted. He read and reread her letter looking for hints that she doubted what she wrote. He remembered Foley and her words on the VFW steps, "Things are better if you read with someone."

But maybe there was more. Maybe Foley. He might return but he'd never get it right. Maybe some smart college guy had spotted her. Or some rich preppie who could be nice until he got what he wanted. Lockett's imagination had run amuck and he knew it, protecting himself from what he didn't know, or couldn't face.

As if she would make those mistakes.

He thought about his father and the snowy afternoon in the Holy Rosary gym.

"You will betray or be betrayed."

He shook his head. He heard himself say: "No."

A few months earlier he had spent most of a day studying street artists in Tokyo before he chose an old painter who held her black and white graduation photo by its corner like a delicate piece of silk. He pointed to her mouth and smiled. Two nights later, Lockett hung the painting inside his locker door. If it meant anything, it should remind him about caring and understanding and what he left behind. He missed his friend.

Gradually, the Navy became an adventure in healing, if healing was the right word. He was sure some growth had taken place. Three square meals a day had added nearly a dozen pounds.

By early 1960, traveling home had become his new compass. The years had changed him enough to know that, like the sea, the future could be complex. He had hoped to visit Lucque, to have a conversation, to ask questions that Lucque would understand and enjoy answering. He had become more curious about emotions and other places inside himself, especially the sad and beautiful ones he had questioned since her letter. Maybe that's what being happy was all about. You don't see it up close. You feel it but you can't get it back. You only get to choose what to remember or forget. But Lucque had left the priesthood and settled in the North Carolina hills where the nearest town was three hundred people and twenty-two miles away.

He was sure a slower trip would help him bleed into civilian life. Thumbing was something he hadn't done since St. Ignatius.

He watched each time another dock faded away from some exotic port that Molly might have called dreamy. He heard the reassuring hum of the ship's twin diesels and watched bow spray and prop wash from waters he would never sail again. He smelled the sting of salt air for the last time the morning the ship entered Pearl Harbor.

For thirty-three months, Ben Michael had been his best friend. Michael had reenlisted at twenty-four after working tug boats out of Port Angeles.

"I couldn't make enough money," he said. "That made her miserable. By the time I realized how miserable she was, she was screwing her boss. Divorce was the best thing that ever happened to both of us. I'll do twenty, maybe work with kids."

Other divers agreed, the Paul Newman look alike gambled below water, but he was still the best diving partner.

"Leave on a Sunday," he said. "Drivers have less traffic and more time to decide. Bright colors make you easier to see. Home man, like your first love, or your best dog. At first I thought I could go back. You forget what life was like there, it doesn't have the same meaning. You're the thing on the other shore now. People are gone, married, changed. Book it, it's like Port Angeles, you can't go home again, man. That's just about everybody's story."

He slapped Lockett on his back.

"I know what you're thinking, you think it's love. There's a price for that. It was one winter night, you fell in love and you still want it more than anything else in the world. You're like the guy who wants to make fifteen minutes of fame last forever. Great smile, eyes, gonna live happily ever after, a whole slew of things. She got into your head, man. You left her and you're still trying to please her. You never even got her into bed, still trying to lay a ghost. Anyway, if you find her, you won't be able to chase her anymore."

He put his hand on Lockett's shoulder.

"Never mind. It's always the chocolate chip you're not eating that tastes best."

He paused. He looked across the harbor at the Arizona monument next to Ford Island.

"A man could travel the world that way, I suppose."

Captain Rex Sather had boarded the two hundred thirteen foot rescue ship days after Lockett arrived from Norfolk. From the beginning, Lockett admired what he thought a college education should feel like, something he never got from young officers trying too hard. Older crew members talked with respect about the decorated commander. Someone called him "a warrior with a feminine side."

Sather sat straight in his chair the morning Lockett left the ship for the last time. He looked serious.

"The deal with you and that bunch in the mess hall," he said.

Lockett swallowed a laugh at "that bunch."

"Yes, sir?"

Sather grinned.

"They're wrong. That's all I'm going to say."

He talked about paying attention to history. He said the Vietnamese had driven out the Japanese and the French, and the U.S. would be next.

"We serve the flag but the flag has a duty to us too," he said, "and that's not clear this time. A lot of good young men are going to die for a few old men's bad ideas. It's about nationalism for them. It's arrogance for us. We shoot their elephants with rocket launchers. Elephants as enemies because they carry rice? That should tell us who we are."

He bent forward and rested his elbows with his hands under his chin. He changed the subject.

"Life rarely works out the way we plan, Lockett. Sometimes a man loves a woman and it's like the first long cruise, the lessons you learn can make a second cruise very rewarding. Think about that. You're pretty absorbed. She may always be like that for you. Some things die, it becomes obvious to everyone but the one who feels saddest."

He looked up and paused.

"Unfortunately, some things stay with us. I lost a fiancé once. It's difficult to let go of someone that beautiful. The problem isn't that things like love don't last. The problem is that they do. It's okay to care that much. To be sad means we gave a damn. But you may be spending time on a version of something that existed, instead of building something new. What are you trying to prove? Who are you trying to impress? Those are questions I couldn't get out of my head for a long time. Only you can answer them now."

He lifted his fist to his chin.

"A tree hung with apples talks about God's plenty. The same is true with pretty women. My experience has been that the more you learn about that tree, the less you'll be afraid to let go and pick another apple. That won't come from any classroom."

He stood.

"It's important to live as completely as we can. None of us wants to die. But we shouldn't do anything to challenge what living requires. I've got twenty years in on October tenth. My family home is outside Charleston. I'm going to build a sailboat and take some art classes."

He watched an outbound destroyer in the channel.

"I was on that ship once," he said. "Good duty. This war will be different."

Sather may have been right about the war. But what he said sounded ambiguous. There had been something almost glorious about watching pretty girls smile and old men stare at his uniform. He remembered returning a left-handed salute from the one armed guy in Chicago's Union Station. He had grinned at sailors from proud fighting ships who looked enviously at the "E" patches on his shoulder, the ones that said he was a crew member on the only ship in the Navy to win three consecutive awards as the best of its kind. He thought about layovers in Norfolk and Chicago and all the double takes when he saw someone he thought looked like Molly.

The grief Sather referred to happened after a Harry Belafonte concert when Lockett returned to the ship with a young cook named John Henry Bird.

Their friendship went back two years when the crew lined up for inoculations before a dozen foreign ports.

Lockett had been surprised when shipmates looked puzzled at them together. His Grand Lac experience had been with Indian friends. He had no Negro classmates in Grand Lac, certainly none in the seminary. What he knew best was that Negros were better boxers. And John Henry knew music.

Bird turned in the line.

"Mr. Oliver, you gonna catch me?"

They laughed until Bird fainted when the corpsman stuck the needle in his arm. Two minutes later he opened his eyes and smiled.

"Thank you, Mr. Oliver."

Lockett repeated what he had said before: "You can drop the mister John Henry."

John Henry said no, it worked well in Birmingham.

"Makes everybody more comfortable."

The Navy had integrated in 1948, but some white sailors kept prejudices and repeated racist remarks like the one that said John Henry was so black he was purple. "Full blooded nigger," they said. For eighteen months, Lockett had listened to four dull eyed drop outs brag about home towns and mangle the language.

"Everbody got exac' same last two names back there. You either named Simpson or Jones or married one. All of 'em knows the other."

Michael had called them "porcine, too much inbreeding, eyes too close."

An hour after the concert, the fat faced Alabama seaman stood as Lockett and Bird entered the mess hall. Three others bunched up behind him.

"Liberty with a nigger? Fuckin Yankee."

Lockett thought about his first Shore Patrol with an old Quartermaster Chief.

"Some animals didn't evolve because they didn't learn fear," the Chief said. "We're on the planet to evolve, but out here, always be ready for trouble. It's not what happens, it's what you do with it. Never say more than what's needed. Remember, you've got the baton, keep it in your off hand. You may need it and your good one too."

But tonight there was no baton, and a fight could delay getting out. Talk had already started about bonuses and extending enlistments for sailors with electronics specialties like his. And their sister ship was in some place called the Mekong Delta.

Tonight might come down to a different lesson. They should remember that he and Bird outranked them and show respect, if not fear, but they were filled with more adrenaline than common sense. He could try a bluff. One or two might buy. And the fat guy wasn't going to whip anybody by himself. Lockett ignored him. He looked at the other three.

"What are you doing with this fat fuck?" he said. "You three will end up doing all the fighting and then the brig. You're embarrassing yourselves for him. You're better than his bullshit."

The fat one took a step forward then stepped back and gripped the table. The tall blond from Shreveport cocked his head, trying to make confusion look like patience. The Georgia guy chewed a fingernail. The other one stared at the fat guy.

A kind of basic mercy switched on and John Henry looked almost amused.

"Man, ain't no reason to fight for no reason. You want some? We gonna get some ice cream. We be right back."

He motioned to Lockett.

Two sat down. Then another one.

Bird carried a five gallon tub of chocolate ice cream from the freezer. Lockett followed with six bowls and spoons and a scoop. Bird filled each bowl with three scoops. The Shreveport dropout smiled. The fat one cracked his knuckles and looked uneasy. He looked around and sat down. The others relaxed. Ten minutes later they stood. Someone muttered, "Thanks."

"Know them boys," John Henry said later. "Hurt people hurt people, don't want to be lookin' bad. Some of 'em come from bad places."

Lockett nodded. Ironically, John Henry and Sather had taught the same lesson: "Ain't no reason to fight for no reason."

An hour later, Lockett fell asleep thinking Molly would have enjoyed the concert.

Goodbye at the gangway almost left room for tears. These were men he never would have known, shaking hands, slapping backs, waving, the kind of camaraderie that developed between men who took a special pride together on a ship. They were young, but they knew they would never see each other again. More than once he heard, "You're gonna miss us."

Michael stood in front of a group holding a new, green, alpaca lined foul weather jacket.

"A bunch of us took up a collection," he said, "that old one of yours won't be much good where you're headed. We'll ship this."

Lockett stepped off the gangway. He walked to the end of the pier and looked back, the same feeling he had with the old cassock, leaving a part of himself behind.

Michael had moved to the bow.

"Show time," he called.

Maybe the best way to leave a friend, Lockett thought, was to be the one leaving, not the one left.

They never said goodbye.

Molly again.

BEYOND BEGINNING

"Every new beginning comes from some other beginning."
Seneca, *A History of Roman Affairs*

On a sunny Sunday, in mid August, 1960, Lockett put on khaki's and an orange and black striped shirt like the one Belafonte wore at the Waikiki Shell. He discovered he had shipped his Ray Bans by mistake. What the hell, Charles Bronson looked confident squinting into the sun.

Two hours earlier, an old Warrant Officer signed his Navy release papers on Treasure Island and dropped him off at the 80/580 split on his way home to Berkeley.

Lockett carried a small black gym bag packed with socks, underwear, toothbrush, shaving gear and a long-sleeved white shirt for after dark. In the middle, he cushioned the small cross Molly made four years earlier using silver solder with driftwood from Dutchman's Creek.

"Remember me," she said.

He thought about the days before he enlisted not knowing much about oceans except on postcards. But the sea had taught him everything from wars that started before they were declared, to sake hangovers where he'd learned another circle of Dante's hell.

August through November of 1959 had been the south Pacific's stormiest in a decade. After nineteen days at sea, his ship docked in Okinawa for three days of rest. That night, he and Michael spent five hours eating dried squid off sidewalks and washing it down with skunky Sapphoro beer. They ordered sake and Kokuryo steak at a nice restaurant. On their way back to the ship, they mixed peanut butter and tuna sandwiches with more sake. It hadn't cost much but it was money that should have been sent home.

Around two that morning, the ship was ordered to search for a sinking Panamanian freighter. Two story swells from typhoon Charlotte mixed with winds that reached one hundred knots. Lockett vomited for thirty-six hours before Michael brought hot chocolate and saltines to his bunk.

"Sake tasted good going down though didn't it," he said.

On the third day, the ship learned it had been given search coordinates sixty-five miles from the freighter's last position. They called off the search. But he had paid a price for thoughtless spending.

Weeks later, in the Philippines, he drank enough San Miguel to tilt a seventeen day old balute to the sun and eat it anyway. More than once, shipmates warned about bar girls who ate a banana or prayed the rosary while they were turned into recreation with a crucifix on the wall above their head.

"All technique," Michael said, "windup toys. The odds are good, but the goods are odd. It doesn't make sense to us. But she's usually the only one who earns enough to support her whole family even after some pimp cheats her out of her cut."

Lockett had watched Formosan rats, big as cats, jump seventeen inch rat guards because people in Kaohsiung ate the cats.

He had witnessed a dozen deaths at sea, like the third class boatswain's mate in the decompression chamber who died from the bends with a forced smile on his face.

He'd said "I'm broke" to beautiful Eurasian women at Hong Kong's Peninsula Hotel in slit skirts with thighs that made him think even more about survival. No wounds, no medals, but he'd seen life aboard a ship that did things and went places most sailors couldn't spell.

He might have taken the train again, like three years earlier after school in Norfolk, trading East Coast doo wop for West Coast folk, Dion and the Belmonts for the Kingston Trio.

"Passengers will please refrain from flushing toilets while the train is in the station."

Or he might have flown all the way to Minneapolis again, like Christmas, 1958, when an Air Force friend smuggled him aboard a MATS flight from Hickam. But his buddy got out and went to dealer's school in Las Vegas.

The flight arrived early in Minneapolis just in time to board the Grand Lac train. He tossed his bag in the overhead rack and ignored the older man seated next to him talking about bibles and commissions. He watched snow covered cattails in marshes replace what seemed like one long season in Hawaii.

A hundred and fifty miles later, he kept his peacoat open as he left the Great Northern depot. He walked with his chest out in a light snow. He passed six Christmas wreaths and a large lighted tree in the Studebaker show room. A block later, a new brown and tan Chevrolet hardtop stopped as he entered the crosswalk. Fats Lund rolled down his window.

"Hey sailor, my sister, three dollars?"

Lockett laughed.

"Nice car. That's too high."

Fats had been gloomy the day Lockett told him about joining the Navy: "Clear says you'll be lucky if she's still here when you get back."

"Quick, get in," he said, "throw that bag in the trunk. Molly's walking up Belknap."

Two minutes later, Fats took a left into the alley between fourteenth and Belknap. He stopped the car and blocked the sidewalk.

"Get down," he said.

He opened his door as Molly turned the corner. He stepped out and waved.

"Hey, Molly, need a ride?"

"Hi Clarence. I was just going…"

Lockett sat up.

"Oh! It's you," she said, "it's really you!"

Fats smiled, "I brought you Ishmael."

Lockett opened the passenger side door. They hugged for a long time after a long kiss.

"I was going for new lipstick before you came," she said.

Lockett explained the change in the plane schedule. Fats squirmed. A tear ran down his face. He would reward himself by telling this to everyone he knew.

As he drove, he talked about his new job as an apprentice pressman, how he thought nobody would work with him after he came out. He laughed when he said it worried him until the foreman told him everything would get easier if he lost weight.

"He told me it would show how much I wanted to be part of the work. So I lost ninety pounds. He seems happy. He was right."

Molly squeezed Lockett's hand and reminded Fats they hadn't seen each other in more than a year.

"Everybody at school was happy when Julia was elected to the Homecoming court," she said. "She's so pretty We know how hard she worked to lose weight."

Fats parked alongside Molly's house. She leaned over and gave him a short hug.

"Merry Christmas, Clarence."

At the back door, Lockett cradled her head in his hands. He dropped his hands to her hips. He kissed her softly, then harder.

"I've never wanted anything like this more," she said.

The snow fell harder.

Later, Lockett wondered where Fats had learned about Ishmael. Some things had changed.

But he still had two years left in the Navy.

Christmas Eve, Molly wore a red wool dress with a classic round collar, long sleeves and a flared skirt. The usher worked hard to focus above her chest.

The day before his leave ended, Lockett's father surprised him and asked about "a drink on your way out." His eyes watered when Lockett said yes. He told Molly that Lucque would have called the invitation, "redemptive power." He didn't say it, but he was not ready to introduce him to her. Molly said she understood, "redemptive power."

Lockett was certain his father knew it was railroad payday when he parked in the full lot behind the Spinning Wheel. The old Irish bar walls featured a five foot long fiberglass muskie and everything that was ever hunted in the woods around Grand Lac. The owner made a show of greeting his old friend and poured three shots of vodka.

"Drinks are on me," he said, "a toast to you both."

Lockett's uniform brought smiles from veterans of World War Two, and Korea, and some of his father's old customers. He watched a kind of Irish charm that must have been a key to his father's business as he came alive making introductions. He thought about men who became softened by age and dreams that failed, how unhappy and ashamed his father must have been without that identity. His bar was where he worked out his problems, where he found worth before he woke to what he didn't think would ever happen. He did the only thing he knew, nurse his anger and hide to avoid more embarrassment.

At the depot, his father seemed unusually quiet. He stared past Lockett as if looking for the right words before they shook hands.

"I'm not you, Oliver," he said. "I know that."

Lockett reached out and touched his arm.

"I'm glad we had the drink. I know who you are. Don't feel sorry."

He tightened his grip on his bag. He boarded the train that had been put together fifteen minutes earlier across the bay. He put the bag above a seat in the middle of the cold coach. His mind drifted. Maybe in his grief, his father was like other men who wanted their sons to set their sights higher, to leave Grand Lac like he should have when he was younger. He had loved at a distance, but maybe the visit to the bar had erased some of that. In an ironic way, his father had been like the missionaries and had done him a favor.

He shivered at the thought of love at a distance. For a hundred reasons, Molly should have been at the depot.

Less than an hour later, a green Ford slowed and pulled

over. A red-haired man who might have been thirty, leaned across and rolled down the passenger side window. He asked where Lockett was going.

"Wisconsin, sir."

Peter Ficke introduced himself and said he pulled over after he spotted Lockett's short hair and Navy dress shoes. He was driving straight through to Cheyenne except for supper. He asked if Lockett was comfortable with that, and if he had a license. Lockett said, "Yes sir."

Ficke said he could get him about half way and added, "You can stop calling me sir."

Navy talk started almost at once. Lockett knew his experiences were as fresh as they would ever be. He took pride telling about what his ship had done.

"But you still learned new ways of dying."

Ficke looked puzzled. Lockett told him about the old diver who pulled him aside and explained "the zone," when you stopped caring after you had done your best.

"You never got used to not getting used to it."

He gave examples of how quiet it got when the ship recovered bodies, like the time the two Air Force pilots collided north of Hokkaido and only one body was recovered. And the Marine pilot who crashed off Coronado, when it took an extra day to find him because currents carried his body from where he went down. He described the looks when divers brought the body aboard covered with shrimp.

"Cook's stopped serving shrimp for a few months."

He talked about Christmas Day in 1958, and the attempt to rescue three Korean Marines who pounded on the bulkheads until they drowned when their compartment was locked and flooded to keep the rest of the ship from sinking.

And New Year's Eve, the next year, in the Taiwan Straits, when they found bodies of three Keelung fishermen who drowned after their boat capsized in eight foot swells and freezing weather. Sather was ten minutes from ending the search when a lookout spotted a body draped across a wooden crate. They pulled a teen aged fisherman aboard and wrapped him in warm blankets with hot water bottles. They dressed him in small sizes of new Navy work clothes and fed him warm fluids and rice and tuna. Michael collected nearly two hundred Taiwanese dollars from the crew who knew the ship wouldn't return to Taiwan at least for another year.

"As much as he'll make in six months," someone said.

At four o'clock the next morning, the corpsman found the fisherman on his hands and knees, scrubbing the deck with a new shirt, apologizing as best he could for getting it wet when they brought him aboard.

What Lockett didn't mention were three missions that began after the ship added a landing craft and two new rapid fire machine guns. For six months they loaded small groups of men dressed in black with giant back packs before the ship left from some obscure port in the middle of the night. A few years later the same groups would be dropped off at the same points in the Mekong delta and called Navy Seals.

Lockett smiled as he told about the young Catholic ensign from Boston College who confused priapism with an exotic disease after he lost his virginity to a Philippine whore.

"The doc called her vigorous. It was a lesson for most of us."

Lockett finished. Ficke turned his head. He said he left the Navy after NROTC at San Diego State and two years of shore duty in Long Beach.

"Of course," he said, "that was five years ago but what you've done, that's very different from being an officer, the experience, officer, you know, enlisted, different. What I mean is, we're both Navy. You signed up, like the guys who get drafted. I had a degree and I don't quite see how that gives enlisted any real idea..."

He hesitated.

"That's all different now, Peter," Lockett said.

Ficke shifted in his seat. For a few minutes they didn't talk.

They said goodbye on the eastern edge of Cheyenne. The radio played rhythm and blues. Twelve hundred miles, and KFCK was the first station they remembered.

The sun was just coming up. The light drowned out the color of the plains. He stopped to listen to a slow freight passing until he couldn't hear it. Dreams are like that he thought, what we know even when we can't hear it any more.

He was tired. His mind wandered.

He could almost hear her breathing. He imagined her asleep somewhere, her back as lovely and natural as the red orange sun. Soon, she'd change into a sheer summer dress for the day. If it were next month, he would hunt until he found her on her campus. He would hear the bell ring after class and walk her to her apartment. They would talk about school and sit on her bed and then talk about

90

her new friends. They would talk more and remember, until they kissed.

It had been two years and he still risked thinking like that. Nipples and long legs, he had become what Joyce had written: "Mr. Duffy lived a short distance from his body." For all he knew, hunting her down would cross territory he couldn't uncross. She might be under some other guy right now. He hated his imagination and how much he was in her power. There was probably some name for it. So what.

And a man might turn into someone else, waiting. Fuck it, so what. But the heart never forgets.

He thought about the jackass.

A year earlier, someone had complained about the food aboard ship. A cook told a story about a guy who bought a donkey that was costing him too much to feed.

"So the guy decides to feed the donkey less and less to make up for his losses. Finally the donkey is down to one cup of grain a day. The plan looks like it was working until the donkey died."

The guy called it a shame.

"If the donkey had lived, I could have gotten him down to nothing."

The cook told the guy he might be a jackass but he should be glad he wasn't the donkey.

A man could live a life like that, Lockett thought, a jackass, trying to make up for a mistake with nothing to show for it.

Cheyenne to Dubuque took the rest of the day. Twenty mile rides left him stranded with barns and weather vanes and middle fingers from hayseed looking teenagers in old pickups. Farm towns along the new interstate looked ordinary or deserted.

Around seven, he watched a hawk circle in an updraft. A Dubuque police car passed and doubled back. The young cop asked the usual questions, name, destination. Lockett showed his driver's license and Navy I.D. He gave details about his trip. The cop scolded him for violating local ordinances against hitch hiking. He repeated it when he dropped him off in a motel parking lot on the other side of the city. The faded blue neon sign read Prairie View Motel. Lockett thanked the cop and paid the three dollar room fee. The old mom and pop motel turned out to be clean and comfortable and quiet.

In the morning, he waited for a drizzle to end. He ate a warm cinnamon roll and drank a cup of coffee in the lobby. He thought about his ride with Ficke, how they hadn't agreed but had done what they both needed. Maybe that's what happened with Molly. Maybe that was the way it should be. He waited with a second cup. The drizzle stopped and he walked the half block to the ramp on to sixty one north.

Lockett had just stuck his thumb up when an old couple stopped.

"Yup, you betcha, goin' up ta Hermantown. Get in, drop ya right next ta da bridge ta Grand Lac der, catch da bus across, too. We're da Heino's. Ya got a name? Gonna get cold in another forty-five days. Live der?"

Lockett introduced himself. He repeated what he told the cop. He smiled at the local version of intimacy when the woman reached over and ran her hand across the old man's shoulder. Molly would have liked that.

"Reino here, he was in da big one, weren't cha honey?"

"Yup," the man said. "Tried ta stay out da way of da Germans and da Russians we did. Thirty below. Speed and skies better dan der guns and boots."

He paused.

"War ain't no good for no one, no sir, just ain't. Ya got a future der?"

Lockett was unsure about what to say. What he wanted was clarity. He gave a slow nod.

"I think so."

By the time the old Finn dropped him off, the mid-afternoon wind had shifted. The temperature was ten degrees cooler on the Grand Lac side of the bay. He thought about Michael's warning: "You forget what life was like there. It doesn't have the same meaning." In a strange way, he had chosen to come back to a black and white place without Molly, like one of the Iowa farm towns without much preserved.

The house smelled like fresh bread. New linoleum had been laid in the kitchen. The back window to his bedroom was open to let out last minute paint fumes. His mother set the dining room table with her China and cooked pork chops, fresh green beans and mashed potatoes with gravy. She had baked the favorite dessert he had nearly forgotten, key lime pie with a graham cracker crust.

Underneath it all was her unconditional love, whatever he had done, however thoughtless or selfish he had been. Before she slept tonight, she would work her rosary beads with the Joyful Mysteries in thanks for her first born son's safe return.

A little after ten, Lockett closed his eyes. The idea of home still included thoughts about being important to someone. He imagined Molly's grey house down the street.

DISSONANCE

"If every plank on a ship is replaced is it still the same ship?"

Plutarch, *Vita Thesie*

Lockett unpacked his seabag on Thursday. He kept the pea coat and two black wool turtle necks. He found his Ray Bans tucked inside a shoe. Ficke's comment about the other shoes landed them deep in a bedroom closet. The rest would get use somewhere along the line.

On Friday, he finished lunch around twelve thirty. He walked past Molly's house, the kitchen, the library, her bedroom upstairs in the back. He swallowed a weak smile remembering her freshness, as happy as he could be.

It had been Grand Lac's hottest summer since 1939. Roses that survived severe winters might not get through the summer. A block away, someone was mowing. Otherwise, people stayed inside with their table fans on high and shades closed, waiting for the newspaper. Tonight they would read the obituaries and practice the local art of small talk: "Your sister's grass was still lookin' good yesterday." "They say it might rain Sunday." "I finished the man's arm on the puzzle last night."

He sidestepped tar that bubbled from cracks where old roots pushed up concrete. He passed through mixed neighborhoods and dying boulevards. Lilacs had mixed with old silver beach. Branches had held robins nests in the summer and made cracking sounds in the winter. He remembered a time when the city had been photographed for postcards, when fog horns and tugs and boats and trains whistled about a community.

Erotic snapdragons still pushed through picket fences. Old lilac bushes still bent, heavy with purple flowers. First growth pines still dominated hundreds of acres in parks that gave residents something in common. Other than that, nothing was impressive enough to tell anyone much about where they came from or how they got there.

The decline began a decade earlier when the iron ore ran out and a waste rock called taconite replaced it. About the same time, railroads changed from steam engines to diesels and jobs were lost. Western states learned it was cheaper to ship grain and coal on barges to New Orleans. Grand Lac lost its economic base, and some say its character. Businesses boarded up. City officials tore down classic old theaters for parking lots and bars. They cut themselves off from the rest of the world even more when they ignored urban and regional development and handed out liquor licenses like penny candy.

"We don't need Fed money controlling us here." "A place with stockyards is worse." "Bars and convenience stores sell liquor and pay taxes."

"Unemployment like an unruly dog," someone said. "You can't beat the door down to get out of here, that door rotted away a long time ago."

Lockett thought about modest, hard-working people with hearts and souls, who took pride in shoveling sidewalks or helping a widow clear hers, who supported good schools and watched each other's children dance in leaf piles and go home when the street lights came on. But the city had become the frog in the pot. The heat gets turned up slowly and the frog never knows until it dies.

Two men in wool suits shuffled with heads down toward the used car lot across the street from the Buick dealer's showroom. Lockett heard the flat northern Wisconsin accent when the tall one with the mustache said something like, "How do people in the south live there anyway?" The short one spit in the middle of the street and stopped to watch it dry. The tall one was Ron Olsen who married Mavis Stark who lived next door after her parents died in an automobile accident south of town during the war.

She was the special one, first in her class, the pretty one all the boys wanted to date. Before she finished high school, people said she had "one of those college girl shapes," she would go places with her looks and brains.

Lockett was seven or eight when Mavis came home the summer after her senior year working with war refugees in places called Latvia and Estonia. She had graduated from a small liberal arts college in Minnesota with majors in French and cross-cultural studies. She talked about the September job waiting for her in Minneapolis called outreach manager for non-profits. She had always been different.

Neighbors watched when Ron picked her up in his yellow, 1931, Buick roadster. He was the first real boyfriend they knew about. He was older and had a good job selling cars at the dealership. They guessed she must have become his inspiration, or maybe Ron had convinced her that life could be a bigger adventure if she stayed. They married that fall. People said it again, she had always been different.

Lockett had seen Mavis at the Presbyterian church on Christmas Eve. She was still pretty. She had one job then, to be a "good little woman," one of "the gals," the price for not doing what she might have been born to do. Fall in love, fall in line.

Maybe, like other residents, she grew old so fast she never understood what she missed. How can you know much more than where you are when you wake each morning next to a man thinking the highlight of his year after deer season would be two weeks in Brownsville, or Kingman, or The Villages? But they probably never forgot the year they went wild and bought tickets to Disneyland. After they saw what they wanted, they bought souvenir pins and Mickey Mouse ears as reminders. They probably still had fun talking about it.

A few minutes before five every Friday, Ron and his friend would order bar brandy and water during Dago Dan's happy hour down the street. They would toss peanut shells on the floor and Ron would talk about the silly little Japanese cars with cheap prices and how they wouldn't last in Grand Lac winters. After the second drink, they would talk louder about imported cars. Once a month, Ron would order three and let go of his idea about ever owning the Buick dealership. Doctors, lawyers, and the Toyota salesman would relax with a dry martini at the Uptown in the next block.

Tonight Ron would stop on his way home from Dan's and buy chocolate covered cherries at the People's Drug where he knew the pharmacist. He'd be more excited than Mavis when he fixed her gin and tonic with the special tonic and hand her the chocolates while she made his favorite Friday supper, baked salmon loaf with white gravy. He would have one more brandy if he didn't have to drive to the air-conditioned theater in Duluth for their Friday night movie date.

A block later, Lockett watched a monarch butterfly land with its wings open on a batch of purple flowers in front of the Nottingham grocery. A thin young woman stood naked from her skirt up in the open second story window above the entrance. He tried not to look when she raised her arms to catch a breeze, but she smiled back. She pressed her fingers against her breasts that showed more than a man's hands could cover. She glanced over her shoulder as if someone behind her said something. She dropped her hands and disappeared.

Some things don't happen because other things do.

He looked at the store entrance and remembered another young woman with another smile from another season. In a few months, the north wind would shake the leaves the way it did in November, his junior year in high school, when he left after a first hour English test, juggling unfinished ideas about St. Ignatius, not belonging with new classmates, embarrassed by his father's unemployment going into its third year and no one to talk to.

He knew he frustrated the nuns who said he wasn't "living up to his potential." Especially Sister Felicity who taught his father in grade school and never forgot it. At least that's what Lockett thought when she frowned after she asked him his father's name the first day of school. And Sister Cecelia, the gentle one who seemed the most concerned. She called him "vulnerable" and added, "You find happiness from people you can count on, then you have to hang on to it. You may not find it the way you expect."

He couldn't remember what he traded for it, but he remembered the red nylon jacket like James Dean wore in

Rebel Without a Cause, where Natalie Wood was an example of God's good taste, and the car went over the cliff. At some level, the jacket guaranteed a defense against being alone. Fuck 'em, whatever they thought.

A few minutes later, Don Wells whistled. Lockett stopped and pretended to tie his shoes while the heavy-set Wells struggled to catch up.

"I need to borrow some money from my sister," he said.

"C'mon."

Lockett heard the tree branches.

The apartment was large with blue carpet and cream-colored walls. Silver framed pictures of young women enjoying themselves filled two table tops. Somewhere in the back, a phonograph played "The Song From Moulin Rouge,"..."your lips may be near but where is your heart."

Wells skipped the introduction, but she smiled.

"My name is Abby, nice to see you again."

Lockett remembered her from a football game a few weeks earlier, early twenties, good figure.

She handed Wells a dollar.

"Run to the Nottingham for me will you, Don? Take this, I'm out of cigarettes, tell him they're for me. Winstons."

"I'll be right back," Wells said.

"Please, sit down," she said.

A minute later, he heard water run and a cupboard door close in the kitchen before she crossed to somewhere in the back and called.

"Can you help me with something?"

He moved to a bedroom door. She was facing away, looking out the window. She turned. She lifted her sweater and walked toward him.

"I'm going to change do you mind?"

She tossed the sweater on the bed and unhooked her bra. She took his hands and pressed them against her breasts, long enough to feel hard nipples.

"They're big aren't they? I told Don I wanted to do this. We have time."

She unbuttoned her jeans and wiggled them to the floor. Lockett saw tan lines and part of a green and purple fist sized bruise inside her left thigh. The back of his neck turned hot. Even at St. Ignatius, he'd never felt this overwhelmed.

She grinned and stretched out on the bed.

"It's hard isn't it. I knew you would. Don't talk. I'll help you."

His stomach tightened. It was one thing to know that he didn't know, another thing to touch. He took a step back.

"I'm not thinking like you are. Please, I don't belong here."

She crossed her arms. She looked toward the window for almost a minute.

"Yes, you do," she said. "But maybe not right now."

She swung her legs off the bed and grabbed the sweater. She sat up and took a deep breath.

"Not now. But I think we'll meet again. I hope so. Sometimes we proceed by accident. I really hope so."

Everything got quiet. Lockett backed through the door. He glanced around the living room and sat down.

"Fucking Wells," he mumbled.

Less than five minutes later, an older man in a grey mechanic's jump suit opened the door. Lockett stared at large hands and dirty fingers. The man snarled as he walked past.

"Who's this, Abby?"

"He's one of Don's friends. He just went to the store for me."

Lockett's stomach rolled. The man growled something about an earlier argument.

The story behind the bruise had to be unpleasant. Lockett ran through what could have happened minutes earlier. He looked again at the silver frames, especially the one with two other blonds who could be her sisters. He wished time would speed up.

It seemed like a long time before Wells came back. He smiled as he came through the door. He heard noise from the bedroom and dropped his smile.

"Cigarettes are on the coffee table, Abby. I kept the change. See you later."

He turned.

"C'mon. Let's go."

Wind gusts blew leaf piles along curbs and smelled like fall. They pushed their hands deep into their pockets and walked for a block before Wells said anything.

"Mean, drinks, angry as hell, never listens. He tells her she's lousy in bed. He hits her. We probably saved her this time. If my dad was alive he'd kill him. I should, anyway. He doesn't know, she talked to a lawyer. I'll get the money later."

As they entered the pool hall, Wells elbowed Lockett in the ribs.

"Did you? Did you have a good time? She wanted to do it. She told me to bring you by if I could."

Lockett thought about the shaking branches, how little he knew, how she must feel, her husband, too much religion, and the difference between this and the pretty cheerleader.

He closed the door.

"It's been a good day."

It would be years before he learned the difference between intimacy, revenge fucks, and trite stories about young men who got started with older women.

He never heard how things turned out with her husband. But in 1959, it might have been her and the pictures all over again with three pretty blonds at the Spanish restaurant in Baguio.

Michael watched.

"You gotta get a new filter, man. Don't touch that stuff. It's not playground rules up here, everybody doesn't get a turn. American sailor, some plantation owner's daughter, you'll get us both killed or court martialed."

An old woman with a face the color of grave stones sat in the shade to the entrance of the newspaper wearing more clothes than she needed. She watched him like it added something important to what she knew. Maybe she had once had the same potential as the city.

He turned the corner on twelfth and saw the green sign, Phelan's Bar.

The old mortuary had been built during the '20's with dark panels, cathedral ceilings and marble floors. Four round windows, not much bigger than portholes spread indirect light except in corner booths. He walked past two large commercial fans Phelan used for air conditioning. He smelled the mix of stale beer, old wood and sweat. He smiled at the ancient jukebox with records Phelan kept to provoke complaints about dated music.

John Phelan had dressed the same way for years: white polyester shirt, black polyester slacks, no watch, no rings, no tie. His long white hair drew Tip O'Neil jokes. He prided himself on running a place that never let anyone grab it all. Behind it was a kind of skill for casual conversation. He talked the whole time he worked both sides of the horseshoe shaped bar. Regulars ignored his stream of consciousness comments: "Damned dream, no sleep last night. Dreamed I was a muffler, exhausted."

More than once, he had loaned Lockett and other regulars money to keep them from selling blood for dates. He knew about Molly. He often asked about Lockett's mother.

The place was empty except for the far corner booth. A heavy-set man sat across from a tanned blond in a white cotton sun dress with her back to the door. Phelan smiled and extended his hand.

"So you're out now, eh? In between for a while? Still going to school over here? Be careful, a lot of intellectual mischief."

"I think I can get a degree, John. Anything in that small one cold?"

Phelan's large cooler made tinkling sounds trying to keep up with its thermostat. Regulars knew the repair history that led Phelan into shaky segues away from a customer's choice to a cold brand in the small cooler.

Phelan checked the booth and set a cold Miller's on the bar.

"On me," he said, "when did you get back?"

Lockett told him about hitch hiking. For ten minutes, they talked about the bar and old customers. Phelan asked about Viet Nam. Lockett said something about being glad he was out. He had gone into the world and come back, and while Phelan wasn't saying it, he sensed things had changed enough to stay away from any more talk about the war.

"You really think you can survive here, smoke in a bottle maybe? Some guys never put it back. At least you won't have to read *Mainstreet*."

He raised his eyebrows.

"Not the same place anymore."

Lockett guessed he meant Molly.

"Clear wrote that her father missed Northwestern, John. Is that what you heard?"

Phelan leaned across the bar. He grabbed Lockett's hand.

"She was never the same, Oliver. They wanted a better school. She was just starting college and they had friends there. But I heard she dropped out, married some guy."

He looked unsure about what to say next. He squeezed Lockett's hand.

"She had a baby, Oliver."

Lockett pulled back. His muscles tensed. He felt heaviness in his stomach.

"That's wrong, John. That's completely wrong."

Clear would have known the hurt. He'd have known and told him. He always knew.

"You tell whoever told you that it's bullshit. Tell 'em I told you that John. Do that. Tell 'em bullshit, mean assed bullshit."

Phelan glanced at the couple in the corner, stalling to digest, to make up for a mistake. Like with the larger cooler, he had lost control. The booth was another segue, a clumsy plea, and he knew it.

"You remember Don Wells? That's him in the corner, his sister, nice girl. You'd like her."

Lockett shook his head.

"Maybe later, John, maybe later."

But he looked.

It all came back. For a second, he imagined what she remembered. He bit the inside of his lip.

Wells stood with two empty bottles and stared toward the bar. Phelan leaned into the small cooler and replaced Lockett's empty. Wells smiled as he approached.

"I thought that was you."

He set two empty Budweiser's on the bar and looked at Lockett's Miller's.

"No more Bud, John. Something different. That Miller's cold?"

He turned.

"You out yet, home on leave?"

He nodded as if he understood when Lockett told him about school in a few weeks.

"C'mon over here and join us, my sister will be glad to see you."

Phelan had moved to the other side of the horseshoe shaped bar. He lit a cigarette and tilted his head. His voice was low.

"Be careful, a lot of female there."

Lockett grinned.

"You're funny, John."

Phelan shrugged.

As they approached the booth, Wells clamped his hand on Lockett's shoulder.

"You remember Abby? Jenny is her twin, but what, two years younger, right, Jenny?"

"Four, Don," she said. "She's twenty-six."

Lockett took a deep breath. He hooked his arm over the back of the booth.

"Anyway, people think you're twins," Wells said. "Sometimes I get confused."

Jenny rolled her eyes at the clumsy introduction.

"Please, sit down. How strange, Abby told me."

She said she teased Abby about barely knowing him. After Abby's divorce, they laughed because Lockett was the unlucky one who arrived early.

"She laughed when she said one day you'd meet again. But I really think she was serious. I know Clear. He said you were getting out, so when I saw you I didn't know who you were, and all of a sudden I did. I'll tell her about this."

Lockett reminded her about how lucky they had been with Abby's husband. Jenny said something about Abby still disappointed and still attracted to men who were shy. Wells shook his head and frowned.

"What's that about? Are you saying you never did? All this time I thought...You never? Now I know why she still wants it with you. You never did? Really? Why didn't you tell me, Jenny, all that talk about nothing?"

"Jesus, Don, she's your sister. You sound like a pimp."

She looked at Lockett. She made a face and winked.

Lockett grinned.

"Hat trick, Don. You didn't get the money, you nearly got us killed, and you got the story wrong."

Wells shook his head again.

Jenny said Abby was a nurse at Tripler, in Honolulu. She knew about his ship but it never seemed to be in port. She had fallen in love with her work and the islands.

"We're best friends, would you ever think about going back?"

"I don't think so," he said.

He paused for a second.

"At least not by myself."

Her lips parted, like finding a key under a doormat. They looked at each other. She blushed. Lockett thought about the absurdity.

Wells missed it.

"You ready, Jenny? I gotta go."

"After I finish my beer," she said. "You go ahead. I'll call you tomorrow."

Wells stared at Lockett and extended his hand.

"Jeez, you never did."

He walked away like the whole thing needed more thought. When he got to the door, he turned. He shook his head and smiled.

After that, the conversation loosened and wandered.

"A lot of people who grew up here want out," she said.

"You, coming back, that's different."

She paused. She flipped her hair back.

"Maybe we're all governed by things we don't understand?"

Lockett decided not to spoil what might have been a tease. He explained why he left and why he came back.

They made each other laugh for an hour before he changed whatever the subject was.

"What keeps you here?"

She said physical therapy paid well in Duluth. She had just found the right house, one of the Lagae cottages that people thought were the best built houses in Grand Lac after the war. She described a full finished basement, a big kitchen and rose bush hedges on both sides of the lawn.

She leaned forward and put a hand on his wrist.

"Tell me about the Navy, the different ports."

He thought for minute.

"A friend from San Francisco said the best cities are civil, Hong Kong, Tokyo, they're like beautiful women, they magnify people. Once in a while, they tell us why we live there. He said you never really cut yourself loose from where you start."

He hesitated. How conditional things were, how much depended on time and place.

Like another hot afternoon, the summer before the Navy. The beach at Pattison Park was noisy with small children. Young mothers not long out of college pretended indifference to college boys playing football. He was sure the shapely brunette on her stomach with her bikini top untied heard the college boy when he dropped the ball next to her and said, "I'd like a piece of this." And high school girls with growing breasts busy comparing their bodies to the young mothers and practicing new lessons on curious college boys.

That day they splashed each other before he carried Molly on his shoulders. He could still feel the sand ridges on the bottoms of his feet and the embarrassment when he fell and got water up his nose. Molly laughed. Then they both laughed.

Later, when the sun went down, they spread a striped beach towel on the warm grass above the vacant sand. He remembered the tips of her breasts and taste of sunscreen on her neck and the stories they told with the rest of their bodies.

"If we're always right or good," she said, "God loses track of us."

Maybe the sky just mattered more on days like that, but three years in the Pacific, and he couldn't remember a prettier sunset.

The conversation with Jenny made sense until they both admitted the obvious.

She looked toward the bar before she ran a hand through her hair. She said she had two steaks and a cold six pack and planned to grill at her new place that night.

"Would you be interested? We could continue our conversation, maybe celebrate for Abby. I'll make a salad."

Lockett had arrived alone. To go on alone because there might never be someone like Molly was unknown, but that's what this was about.

They finished the last of their beer and moved toward the door. Her walk reminded him of her sister.

Phelan came full circle when Lockett said goodbye.

"In between for a while? Looks like you're gonna be. You oughta play the lottery."

Lockett grinned at the "I told you so" way Phelan got by with it.

Jenny whispered, "I think he's funny."

The wind off the lake carried the smell of milkweed and burnt grass.

Jenny lit the grill and laid two rib eyes off the center. Minutes later, the juice came through. She cut off a piece and handed it to him.

"I know what I want when we're done," she said.

Later, they took off their clothes. Lockett followed the same shapes and crimsons and tan lines. No green and purple bruise, no hurry.

She tossed her hair.

"If there's no one else to live for," she said, "we live for ourself. Abby will understand. I'll tell her she was right, sometimes we proceed by accident."

In the morning, they woke with the sun on their folded clothes.

"Tell me," he said, "does the same accident happen more than once?"

She pulled the sheet off and stretched her arms over her head.

"Talk to me again," she said.

Lockett laid his hands on her shoulders.

If there's no one else to live for...

CHANCES ARE

"Heard melodies are sweet,
But those unheard are sweeter."

John Keats, *Ode on a Grecian Urn*

In three years as a switchman, Clear had never swept. He explained his idea at Phelan's.

"The car has a broken seal. Somebody's already been there. It's easy to get to, on a siding off twenty eighth."

He figured at least an hour between rounds by the cops.

"We use two cars. We load trunks and take out the back seats. How about Fat's, you and McVitie use your cars? Fitz, you help load. We'll sweep, Oliver. After gas, we should come out with about twenty a piece."

Four years earlier, it would have been a day spent with Molly.

The previous week, Lockett had bought a blue 1953 Chevy with a radio and heater, the one he wished he'd had on cold nights with her. The odometer read ten thousand miles. A car like that was too nice to haul grain.

Most locals knew, boats anchored in the harbor, and boxcars parked on sidings meant grain waiting to be loaded. In 1960, the minimum wage was a dollar. Twenty dollars would help with car payments. But sweeping tested good judgement. Selling it black market to farmers was a felony though nobody thought the railroads couldn't afford to lose a little wheat.

The next day, Lockett buttoned a long-sleeved shirt at the neck. He tied a red bandana across his face to keep from choking inside the boxcar. His eyes watered. Dust mixed with sweat and coated his jeans like butter. He had lost count of the fifty-pound burlap sacks they had cashed at the pawn shop when a ten-penny spike pushed through his tennis shoe into the ball of his foot. Clear spotted the blood.

"We're almost done, meet you at John's."

An old emergency room nun removed the tennis shoe and bloody sock. She cleaned the puncture and asked how it happened. Lockett realized how dirty he was. He assumed the nun had been there long enough to know about sweeping grain. What the hell he thought, he was there for a foot, not a confession.

"I was working on my car, Sister."

She finished wrapping the foot and delayed a second before she looked up.

"You'll need a tetanus shot. I'll be back in a minute."

He waited for a long time before she returned and told him to roll up his sleeve.

"You may need a stitch or two, but let's see how this goes."

She handed him two packages of gauze bandages and two packages of light blue cotton boots the hospital used for patients without slippers. She told him to leave the bloody sock off and wear one of the boots.

"Stay off the foot and use the gauze if it bleeds again. Call your doctor if you see red streaks."

Lockett stuffed the gauze and the three extra boots in his back pocket. Ten minutes later, he replaced the boot with the tennis shoe and bloody sock in front of Phelan's.

Clear bought a beer and explained.

"Cop caught me and Fitz, fifteen minutes after you left. Really pissed. But he knows my mother from church. We didn't crack the seal, so he let us go. Still can't figure how he made rounds that early."

He handed Lockett a twenty and two ones.

"Drivers got a little more for gas."

Phelan reached into the small cooler and muttered something about grown men with toddler's minds. Clear leaned over and whispered.

"Jackie's pregnant, we're getting married, I need the extra money."

Lockett felt the hair lift on the back of his neck. Three or four years earlier, it could have been Molly.

Clear finished his beer and looked down the horseshoe curve.

"C'mon guys, roll you for the next one."

Lockett hadn't played a bowling machine in two years. But machines come back like swimming. He lost the first two games. He won the third. He asked Phelan for more dimes as Midwest Dahl came through the back door with a fat cigar in his mouth. His faded Army green tee shirt showed big biceps.

Midwest had been baptized with the name Stanley after his mother named him Zero when the nurses asked her what she thought of her new baby.

That wasn't the only story people told. Once he had asked if he should pull down his pants after his doctor told him he wanted to check his carotid. Another time he was caught having sex with a dead deer.

The case hinged on the word "living." The law said sex with "any kingdom of living animal beings." Dahl's attorney argued that the deer was a carcass. Since it wasn't alive, it wasn't covered by the law. The judge gave Dahl a choice, one year in jail or two in the Navy. His attorney said Dahl couldn't swim. The frustrated judge sentenced Stanley to two years with the infantry in Korea.

The name Midwest Express came a few years earlier when he disappeared for a year then told everybody he'd been released for good behavior from a minimum-security prison in Huntsville. Texas police told a different story after they found him stocking shelves at a Grand Lac grocery store. He had walked away from the prison and ducked police as a helper on cross country furniture vans. The cost of taking him back to Texas wasn't worth the few months he had left to serve, and Midwest hadn't bounced any more checks like the ones that got him in prison in the first place, so they let him go. But the name Midwest Express stuck.

Months before he left the Navy, Lockett was sure that going back to Grand Lac would mean dreams he should keep and some he should forget. He had nursed the idea that his first days home would be special. And they had been just like that. The grain money helped. Seeing Dahl counted even more.

Dahl grabbed the leather cup and rattled the dice.

"Roll you for a beer, John."

"Joint's not run by the Sisters of Charity, Dahl. Want the beer? Pay the money."

Dahl paid fifteen cents for a Schlitz tap and stubbed his cigar in an ashtray. He squeezed the end and slipped it into his pants pocket. He watched for ten minutes like reconnoitering in the Army before a battle.

"How about a beer and a buck, Clear? Winner take all."

"Sure, Stanley," Clear said, "we'll take your money."

Like a chorus, Fats and Fitz and McVitie said, "I'm out."

Clear turned his back to the bar and whispered.

"Your old buddy. He's pretty good. Left-handed. We'll split."

"Splitting" pretty much guaranteed more income. If Clear won, he'd collect and pay Lockett back later. If Lockett won, he'd collect but repay Clear.

The right side of the machine lined up hard against Phelan's wall. Dahl couldn't take the extra step to his right he needed to roll left handed. He lost three games before he lifted the machine and angled it out from the wall.

Phelan snapped.

"What the hell you doing, Dahl? Break the machine bouncing it around like that."

"I need some room, John, not hurting nothing."

"For Chrissakes Dahl, if I wanted people to have more room, I'd move it myself. Other people don't need more room. Agitated density? Throw the ball right."

Midwest shook his head. "C'mon, John, I'm no good right."

"Right, left, in your case, good got nothing to do with it. Got a hard on? Can't think? Use both hands."

Dahl turned into a child with a lost toy.

"They're gonna beat me, John."

Phelan glared.

"I'm helpless against that genius, Dahl, they're gonna beat you anyway. About time you paid. Remember the last time? Like never?"

He lifted a glass from the sink and held it toward a window.

"Path to enlightenment's never clean, Dahl."

Phelan didn't dislike many. But if you grew up in Grand Lac, you spent time in bars, especially in the winter, and you learned two things: you bought a round when your turn came, and if you cheated, at cards, or dice, or the machines, you spent a lot of time by yourself. Dahl never bought.

Phelan let Dahl keep the machine where he moved it. Later he said he knew he would lose anyway.

Dahl played better, but Clear or Lockett won every time. Dahl quit six games later. Clear reminded him to pay and struck up a conversation with two guys Lockett didn't know. Dahl paid up.

"Haven't seen you for a while," he said. "What ever happened to that friend of yours? The one with the nice tits. I thought she always wanted it. You know what I mean?"

He slapped Lockett on the back with an unnatural laugh, like replaying something funny.

"I heard she got knocked up and moved to Alabama or Texas or someplace south. Sure didn't like the way I danced."

He grinned again before he gripped his glass tight with both hands and swallowed the last of his beer. He licked the rim of his empty glass.

"Good fuck? Ain't that what they're for?"

The Christmas leave at the Billings Park Center came back like probing an old wound. Dahl had asked Molly to dance near the end of a night after a lot of drinking. Lockett knew she would be too gracious to say no. But she hesitated. She turned to him. He smiled and opened another beer.

"That could be interesting," he said.

117

She said yes to Dahl. Seconds later, he pushed hard against her until she broke away and ran crying to Lockett. He shoved Dahl against a wall. But he forgot the rule about not letting up. Dahl's body seemed to swell before he paralyzed Lockett with a knee to the groin. He pulled him down and banged his head on the floor with his elbows.

"Fuckin' Navy boy."

Clear and two others pulled Dahl off. Lockett stood and tried to smile. Molly dabbed blood from the corner of his mouth and behind his ear.

"I'm sorry," she said.

In the background, Fats Domino played, "Ain't That a Shame."

Ideas about a day like this had grown since. Molly's tears had not gone away. Neither had Dahl's foul breath, the flashes of light, and the sour taste of blood.

In August 1959, the waters in the San Bernadino Straits were calm north of Luzon. At three in the morning, Sather talked about the sea as a spiritual mirror.

"None of us wants to die," he said. "But we shouldn't live doing nothing to challenge what living requires. You'll learn, every sea has its own motion. We grow from the same kind of uncertainty. Some things you let go, some things you avenge. The challenge is to find the right way and have it find you, to put yourself in the right place."

After that, Lockett looked for more lessons on nights when she was thousands of miles away and the line between the sea and the horizon was as close as he could get.

"What's wrong with you," Dahl said. "You got something to say? She still botherin' you?"

Lockett stood and pulled his shoulders back.

"I made a couple of mistakes that time, Dahl."

Phelan heard the challenge and cocked his head.

Dahl smirked.

"That so? Things happen, I'm not very good at feeling sorry. That's a fact."

His eyes narrowed.

"Anyway, your foot's bleedin'. You should be glad it's only your foot."

He reached into a pocket and pulled out a toothpick. He picked his teeth and looked at it. He laid it on the bar. Phelan shook his head like he had surrendered.

"You plan to use it again? Philistine provincial. You complicate your life doing shit like that, Dahl, why not just puke there?"

He grabbed a clean towel. "Woefully unsocialized." He squeezed the toothpick like it was diseased. He washed his hands and looked at Lockett, guessing what should have been done that night, and how dark it must have been since.

Lockett took a deep breath. In front of him was what he had arranged for a long time.

"You've always been a prick, Dahl."

Dahl's smirk froze.

"Fuck you."

He stood and cocked his shoulder. His left arm started up. Lockett's right snapped his jaw. He screamed. He grabbed for the edge of the bar like falling off a shelf.

No sense saying it, Lockett thought. He won't be listening. But he said it anyway.

119

"That's so, Dahl."

Phelan tossed his chin in the air and pinched his throat.

"Picnic lightening. Swede, too dumb to be intimidated."

Dahl rolled to his side. He tried to stand. Phelan moved from behind the bar with a twinkle in his eyes.

"Stayin' down could make this the most important day in your life, Stanley. You should be grateful."

Dahl sat back. The gap on the left side of his mouth showed where his tooth had been.

Phelan lifted Dahl and walked him to the door.

"Like I said, Stanley, you complicate your life with shit like this."

He paused.

"Something beautiful about the way a tooth breaks like that."

Lockett stepped away from the bar. He stared at the same knuckles Molly had brushed against with her hip.

"None of us wants to die," Sather had said, "but we shouldn't live doing nothing to challenge what living requires."

Lockett took a deep breath. The thunder in his ears had stopped. The lightening after every blow and the sour taste of blood were gone. He may never see her again, but where ever she was, she could stop crying. Today's truce with himself seemed trivial. But maybe today he'd start forgetting.

Clear raised his eyebrows and broke into a smile.

"Time for some fresh air, Oliver. C'mon, make some more money at Casper's. His machine is more forgiving. Whoever wins, we split."

Phelan listened. His shoulders sagged.

"Heard that before," he said. "Illiterate conceit. Crazies howling at the moon, people with bad breeding hearing dog whistles. Place like that, no good parts. Go there, you win, somebody changes your nose, you lose. Everything out of proportion."

Casper had opened the bar after migrating from Hibbing five or six years earlier with a big injury settlement from the mines. Nothing was ever definite about a tie to the mines. But he had money, and no modesty. He had his hair cut with an appointment once a week on Friday, bought expensive clothes from Dayton's in Minneapolis, built a big house outside Duluth, and drove a new Cadillac.

Grand Lac residents had long memories about where people came from, especially the ones from modest backgrounds who moved up to places like the Knife River without knowing the difference between old money restraint and new money excess. Phelan called it, "what poor people think rich people do."

And Phelan had been right about Casper's. Vulgarity and ignorance made the place a risk. Bikers, wife beaters and town toughs listened as he chain smoked and whined about the one thing people definitely knew: the BB gun he fired when he was ten and hit an old woman in the eye. The eye got infected and the old woman died. The same story, over and over, "When I was younger"…"If only I"…Listening was the cheap price they paid to behave any way they wanted.

Lockett thought about the magical times with Molly in the block between Phelan's and Casper's, businesses that had been in the neighborhood for decades, the theater, restaurants, retail stores, and owners concerned about the

121

city's future who worked along employees until they got old and died. Today the gritty alley was like one of the Iowa towns without a soul, vacant buildings, dirty brick walls, and dust devils pushing empty beer cans north and south. The last restaurant told the story best: the owner died, the food got bland, service turned indifferent and the place stopped serving breakfast. His children announced the closing the day before they locked the doors and left town.

The short walk guaranteed an easier machine and more money. But Lockett's day was about as good as it could get.

"Too much drama, I think I'll stay."

"I still feel lucky," Clear said, "maybe later."

The next morning, Billy Cloutier sat three bar stools away. Between turns on the railroad, he spent hours collecting gossip and trivia from bartenders and waitresses. Phelan called him "The Gazette." He ordered a bag of potato chips and a Miller's.

"John, did you hear the one about the two blonds walking in the woods? They reach a creek and the first one crosses over. The second one hollers, 'How do I get to the other side?' The first one hollers back, 'You are on the other side.'"

Phelan's expression never changed.

Cloutier grinned. He reached over and touched Phelan's sleeve.

"Guess who died last night, John."

Phelan worked for an answer, as if another joke would be worse.

"You'd never guess, John," Cloutier said. "Nix. K.O. Deader than Kelsey's nuts. Tipped over sweeping grain.

Drunk, broke, bitchin' about a headache. Siding up on twenty eighth. Half hour later, boom, dies at the hospital."

"You always want to exit doing what you love," Phelan said. "How'd they get him outta the yard? Christ, need a forklift."

K.O. had been part of a Duluth crowd that drank on the Minnesota side until bars closed, then crossed the bridge to squeeze in another hour playing loose and free at Casper's. Lockett could see his bear like shape, his name tattooed above a large lightning bolt on his right arm, and below a skull and cross bones on his left. A decade earlier, he had been an encyclopedia on dirty fighting in a dozen amateur fights: spin the opponent, scrape the glove's laces across his face, rabbit punches, thumb his eye, punch below the cup. Fights were predictable: knock the guy out early or get disqualified to avoid getting hit, then blame the referee for stopping the fight. Most of all, never take a beating.

Lockett assumed that K.O. was still a full-time bouncer and part time burglar who broke into boxcars with a regular crew of four or five others.

Gazette told how they took K.O. to St. Joe's and how his sweaty body made problems for nurses and orderlies.

"Can you imagine, they're wrestling with a beached whale and, get this, a snub nosed .38 falls out of his pocket. Loaded. Surprised he never used it with that temper. Nun's name is Adorno. Been in emergency for fifty years. Seen sweepers every year. She knows what the dust means. Sweepers tell her the truth, she doesn't call the cops. If she thinks they're lying, she calls. She asks what they're going to use the grain for. Can you see 'em? Shufflin' their feet, lookin 'around? All five guys, two just outta prison, three Catholic. Stealin's alright. Lyin' to a nun—straight to hell. Finally, one guy says it's for his chickens. She knows he's lying. Cops stopped 'em before they got to that all night pawn shop on third. Say it's for a tail light. Probably broke the light before they pinched 'em. Protectin' the nun."

Lockett hid a smile. Sister Adorno had made a phone call to the police while he was waiting for the tetanus shot. No wonder Clear had been confused about how the cop got there.

Cloutier changed the conversation. He asked Phelan if he remembered a guy named Otto Allen. Phelan nodded.

"Haven't seen him in a while."

Cloutier said Allen was supposed to get married in Platteville until he found his bride with the caterer in the back of the cake truck half an hour before the Mass.

"And they weren't eating cake."

A minute later, Clear pulled a stool next to Lockett.

Cloutier repeated the story about Otto Allen.

"Otto Allen disappeared. We were just talking about what happened to him. Nobody knows."

Clear ordered three beers.

"His honeymoon," he said, "book it, Vegas. That's where they were going and he went anyway."

Weeks later, Otto turned up driving a limousine for a wedding chapel in Las Vegas. Clear just knew.

He began talking about the night before at Casper's. Phelan leaned back and muttered something under his breath.

"K.O. Nix watched me on the machine," Clear said. "Said something like, 'Brother you need some competition.'"

They agreed on a dollar a game. Clear won for half an hour. K.O. kicked a wall. Clear thought he might quit, so he told him about the car with the broken seal on twenty eighth.

Clear won for another hour. K.O. missed a split. He called Clear a cheater. He grabbed a pool cue and swung at his head.

"So it's all noise and everything is moving and people are scattering," Clear said. "He's gonna club someone or spear 'em and I think I got the best chance to be the someone. Casper's got a loaded .45 and a softball bat behind the bar. But he's got no idea how to use them. Best chance I had was my feet. I'm backpedaling toward the alley. I grab the cue ball off the table and throw it. I'm off balance but it gets him square in the chest. He grabs for a stool and knocks it over. He slips and falls and I hear him grunt. I'm out the door in two seconds. I look back and see K.O. on his knees in the alley. Casper and some other guys are leaning over him."

"Gull breaks a wing," Phelan said, "fishing days are over. You should know where to spend your money next time. Mean crazy. Beat that poor little Culhane girl, chewed the neck off that wounded duck. Always keep two sets of books on that kind, could have killed you."

Cloutier looked at Clear. He told his story about K.O. dying, again. Clear tilted his head. Somebody had died. Somebody else could have died. He turned on his stool and looked out the windows.

Cloutier slid a dollar across the bar.

"Quarters, John. We need some music."

He paused at the jukebox.

125

"Jesus, John, this shit's old. Johnny Mathis? When you gonna get some new music?"

"Chances are, 'cause I wear a silly grin,
The moment you come into view,
Chances are you think that I'm in love with you..."

The lyrics slammed Lockett. The room spun.

"Listen to the lyrics," she had said. "That's the song I wrote you about. You wrote back the nicest letter. You said that if there was ever a song to make someone know he was in love, that was it."

Phelan opened three Miller's and set a clean glass next to each one.

"A toast to knowing when to quit."

He looked at Cloutier.

"Cops keep the grain?"

Cloutier grinned and rolled his eyes. He finished the potatoes chips.

"What do you think?"

He licked his fingers and left.

Clear stood. He clamped his hands on his waist and stared at Phelan.

"Midwest's not the only one who had a bad day," he said.

He punched Lockett on the shoulder.

"Right?"

Lockett shrugged and looked away.

Forgetting wouldn't start today.

TOO MUCH AND TOO LITTLE

"What if you slept and in your sleep
You dreamed and in your dream
You went to heaven and there plucked
A strange and beautiful flower
And what if when you awoke
You had that flower in your hand
And then what?"

Samuel Taylor Coleridge, *Animae Poetae*

Lockett knew his bowels were shot even before the first Friday, in December, 1970. He hoped he could last fifteen minutes and wouldn't be noticed leaving what senior faculty called "the annual mandatory courtesy," or "the event of the year for fawning flatterers." Nobody talked about missing the Christmas Tea at the President's house.

He thanked the President and his wife and wished them Merry Christmas. He did the same with the two vice presidents then slipped through the kitchen and out the back door. He cringed at the thought of two more uncomfortable minutes inside.

The new Buick was parked as close as he could get, a No Parking zone a half block away. He threw the black wool top coat and blue blazer to the passenger side and slid behind the wheel. He thought about the salesman who convinced him to spend the extra money on cold leather seats. The guy had been right for the wrong reasons.

Ten minutes later, his only thought was to turn the whole mess into something manageable. He left his belt, watch, shirt and tie in a trail from his front door. He emptied the keys, wallet, change and handkerchief from his pockets. He rolled his shorts in the charcoal slacks and tossed them on the shower floor with his socks. He finished his shower and dropped the wet bundle into a garbage bag. The cost of new slacks was less than the price of explaining the embarrassment to old Mr. Sedilla, the dry cleaner.

Monday, Lockett told his new doctor he knew every men's room on campus. His doctor called it irritable bowel syndrome and said some men respond to the same kinds of stress with a rash or ulcers.

"It's unpleasant and inconvenient but it's not fatal. At thirty-two, you should be fine."

He prescribed a bland diet and a bulk laxative.

"Check back in a week if it isn't better."

"Unpleasant and inconvenient" was what Lockett had come to, struggling through the start of a teaching career at Flagstaff.

It may have been luck, it may have been the article he milked from his dissertation and published in a major journal, but he had landed the job at least a dozen others had applied for. His goal was a world away from big university research, to teach like the best who had taught him: the guy with the Ph.D. from Berkeley who rode boxcars during the depression, the man from Yale who fought on Normandy, the ex-Jesuit who taught at the Sorbonne, and the woman who studied under Carl Jung. Pinon College offered a chance to be like them, to pass on ideas, give advice, and reassure the good instincts students were starting to have.

A month earlier, Phelan had mentioned a remark by a customer who said if Lockett could get a Ph.D., anybody could. Lockett knew the guy who married a plain girl to avoid the draft and ended up substitute teaching physical education in northern Michigan after seven years between fraternity parties. He tried to dismiss the whole thing as more bar noise. But it stuck.

A few minutes before eight o'clock on the first morning, he stood in front of the largest of his three classes and watched shadows move across twelve-thousand foot mountains north of the campus.

Twenty-five sleepy faces, deserving of his best, said wake me, better yet, keep me awake. That was Lockett's first challenge, an early morning elective course without much rigor. His other classes might struggle to answer why the richest nation in the history of the world didn't have a national health care system, how a small group could turn democracy into a personality show and strangle it, or why state universities cost so much. But the difference between rigor and value could be taught, and he would stress that.

Six or eight hours of experience subbing for his major professor was enough to know four or five would do all the work well, four or five would drop or do nothing, and the rest would respond in the middle. He'd figure out what would work and what wouldn't.

The roster looked balanced, freshmen through seniors, about the same number of males and females, two black males, two Indian females, a female and three male Hispanics, and a short muscular cop with a mustache. There were two Amanda's. A tall blond named Roe with icy blue eyes and too much sun for her age slouched near the back fighting to stay awake. And a pretty California flower child with smiling eyes in a thin peasant blouse in the front row named Nagle.

He introduced himself. He called the roll and matched the roster with as many faces as he could remember. He passed out index cards that asked for a name, major, hometown and high school to get a better idea about backgrounds. He walked through the syllabus and hit on the high points: Cheating was an F for the semester, comments and questions were to be respectful and respected, baseball caps indoors were signs of bad manners and bad hygiene. He didn't mention what some already knew, the underside of a cap brim was perfect for crib notes.

He had nearly finished when an older girl in a low cut dress and spiked heels crossed in front making it impossible for anyone to stay focused. She moved down the center aisle to the back row, indifferent to the attention.

Lockett pretended to ignore the class measuring his reaction. He shortened his remarks by ten minutes for the inevitable first day questions: "Can I skip during deer season?" "Will tests be mostly from the book or from lectures?" "My mother is getting married again next month in New York. Is it okay if I take off a few days?" "Can I get the assignments before I leave for a ski trip in Europe?" The cop asked if wearing the uniform was a problem and repeated his name, Clyde Murch.

The girl in high heels waited until the others finished. Her wine-colored dress was tight at the waist like a Gunsmoke saloon woman. Lockett guessed late twenties. She introduced herself as Sophie Dowd. She apologized for being late. She had just moved from Las Vegas and this was her first semester. She worked as a stripper and sometimes she worked after hours. She said there would probably be more mornings like this. If that was a problem, she would find another section, or take the class later.

Lockett crossed his arms. He told her she was welcome to stay.

"You might want to check with other students for the notes depending on how late you are," he said, as if she was some kind of rabbit turning multiple tricks that made her late. He bit his bottom lip and rubbed his neck. She smiled but passed. She said she wanted to get a degree, to leave her work behind and get married. She hoped to teach in an elementary school, someplace where nobody knew her, some small town in Idaho or Montana maybe. She said she'd show up on the final roster and she'd be a good student. She smiled.

"I'm good at what I do."

Days with Murch were uneven from the start. Lockett resented the ex-Marine's interruptions and questions that argued ideas based on something he "knew" or "felt." Students added new questions, like squirrels finding nuts, and the original question got lost.

"How can you say we should give inmates a free education," Murch said. "We'd all like a free education. Why reward a convicted criminal?"

Lockett explained that most inmates weren't killers or serial rapists, that no country in the world put more people behind bars and kept them longer, then recycled them out with no training, no education and no job.

"We spend millions for warehousing, then we free them and hope a different America happens."

He emphasized teaching non-violent prisoners how to think, how to get and keep a job, how to cope in a civilized world. Education gave convicts a chance for rewards and reduced the costs for everybody.

"A whole cycle of change is possible. It saves more than it costs."

Murch sat with his back straight and shook his head.

"It saves more than it costs? Excuse me doc, but that sounds like a lot of high-minded sociology bullshit. We don't spend more money on them. We lean on them. That's the world I come from. Justice isn't cerebral."

He rubbed his mustache.

"Would you like to ride with me some night?"

Two weeks into the semester, Lockett had stopped counting the number of times he wanted to tell Murch to do him a favor and shut up. He wasn't interested in learning from a cop, not in the classroom or in his car. Anyway, a ride took more time and energy than Lockett wanted to spend. But the challenge had students smiling. A whole semester was left, Murch might bring it up again, or someone would remember and remind them.

Maybe it wouldn't happen.

"Sure, I'd like that some time," he said.

Five students dropped at the end of the second week. A dishwater blond from Parker scowled and squirmed through every lecture. She took time to scold him the morning she dropped.

"I had better teachers in high school."

It was the kind of challenge his mentors would have overlooked, but she was probably right. He could feel himself intimidated, rushing through material, skipping examples, not pacing for depth or relevancy. His questions had been met with uncomfortable silences. But he pictured her fed up with more than his class, back in Parker, in a hot desert trailer house with no air conditioning, barefoot, pregnant and no degree. At least he wouldn't have to look at her spoil his class.

At the end of September, he returned a simple check test on his lectures and the first two chapters. Most grades were good. Roe may have been bored, but she led the class with a ninety-five. Nagle and Dowd followed with ninety-three's. After class, a Magoo looking freshman named Happ apologized for a sixty-seven and promised to do better. A junior named Morgan fidgeted and laughed.

"I've got to take better notes. This stuff confuses me."

Nagle waited until the end.

"I'm in English and this is my last semester," she said. "I wish I would have taken more sociology."

Lockett complimented her about her grade.

"Thank you," she said.

Her eyes held firm.

"You're not bad."

For the first time someone had responded to his teaching with pleasure. Somebody had felt his effort. He knew better, "not bad" could have meant a couple of things. But it tasted like a success.

"That means a lot," he said.

He forgot what else she said. But her thought was enough.

That night he replayed her message. Like Molly, someone had seen something in him better than he had.

A week later, the morning air turned crisp. Winds began taking down pine needles. Colors changed overnight in the high mountains. The second week in October brought colder temperatures and snow flurries.

Lockett's new lecture stressed the family as a social institution. The text questioned romantic love as a basis for a complex relationship. He hoped the section about different mating patterns would provoke more questions about sex and religion.

"For Friday, your assignment is to examine the meaning of 'I love you.' What is love? What is this thing we fall into? What does it mean for a society? Do love and sex exist independently? No more than a page."

A few faces responded with smiles.

Friday, he said the papers were good, "lots of A's and B's."

"I'm going to read two, don't worry, anonymously. These are not necessarily the best. But they show a range of thought and they're creative, one male, one female. This is not quantum physics. But remember, value and rigor aren't the same, I want to see you think."

The first paper belonged to a senior named Garcia.

"I love you is the feeling I have for the black-haired girl in the third seat from the front on the second row from the windows."

The class laughed. The girl named Casey blushed. Someone muttered, "Good taste."

Lockett looked out the window. He kept his face blank.

"I'll be glad to introduce you after class."

The second paper was Nagle's. She questioned and doubted. He hoped it would stimulate conversation.

"Love is a dream and a privilege," she wrote. "When romantic love happens, it enriches the lives of those who experience it. I love you is a declaration of joy, gratitude and devotion. It usually begins in passion that changes everything. It's new and intense and mistaken for genuine, unselfish love. In the end, is romantic love a special chemistry between two people or a cultural preference? The question is, how do we love after the delight?"

The class went quiet. About half nodded and approved. Jim Eden, the pony tailed hippie from Portland, raised his hand.

"We don't, we spend the next eight years arguing over money."

A senior named Toby Kofman frowned. He cocked his head and raised his hand.

"I'm not impressed with the book, and that's a girl right? How does she think people get married without passion, have families, go to church together, live together for decades? How do we get societies? How does that fit with what she says? Dumb cunt."

Students opened their mouths like air had been sucked out of the room. Dowd shook her head. Some people looked stunned. Males made eye contact with Lockett, as if they were lost. Nagle looked down like a shy animal.

Lockett could practically smell the tension. He crossed his arms and felt the sweat under his shoulders. He saw the cords on Murch's neck stand out as he shot his hand up. To hell with him, Lockett thought, things are messy enough, that's not the way to go. He shifted three steps toward the door and motioned.

"Mr. Kofman, come with me."

The class checked Kofman, then Lockett. Lockett took another step and repeated himself. Kofman stood and walked ahead into the hallway. His red down vest made him look bigger than his two hundred pound frame. Lockett took a last look at the class and closed the door. He walked past Kofman and turned.

135

"What the hell are you thinking Kofman? Never mind. I don't care what you're thinking. We've got a problem and you're going to help fix it. You're going back in there and apologize, first to the young woman and then the class. You don't have to know who she is, you apologize to who wrote it. If you don't, I'll drop you from the class with an F. After that, I'll figure a way to ship your ass back to Shaker Heights. You owe her, you owe them all."

He wished he could have made it more painful, at least as miserable as it had to be for her. He wasn't sure about the F, much less the part about Shaker Heights.

Kofman pressed his chin against his chest. His shoulders were hunched. His arms hung loose at his sides. He stuttered and cried.

"I'm very sorry…I'm very sorry."

"That's a start," Lockett said. "You should be ashamed. You know better. Someday, somebody's boyfriend is going to kick your ass for a remark like that. If you're really sorry, if you get it right, you'll learn a good lesson. You owe that to yourself."

"I don't have an excuse," Kofman said. "I'm discouraged about a lot of things. My parents want to know what I'm going to do when I graduate. So does my girlfriend. I don't know."

The world slowed.

"Whoever wrote it shouldn't pay for that," Lockett said. "Take a minute, you'll be fine."

He remembered the universal caution: "They may not like who you punish, but if you violate one, you violate them all."

He glanced through the door window. Nagle looked frail and sad.

A minute later, they reentered the room. Lockett felt the anxiety. Nagle's head was bowed but she had stopped crying.

"Mr. Kofman has something to say," he said.

Murch raised his hand before Kofman got his first words out. Lockett ignored him again.

"I'm sorry," Kofman said. His voice cracked.

"I apologize, to everyone, especially to whoever wrote the paper. I was wrong."

Nagle looked up.

"I wrote the paper, Toby."

She stood. Kofman hesitated before he stepped toward her. She extended her hand. The bell rang. Garcia chatted with Casey.

Monday, Nagle slowed as Lockett gathered his notes after class.

"Thank you for Friday," she said. "Poetry doesn't always tell the truth but it should show what's beyond feeling, to see through things, including ourselves. The assignment gave me a chance to do that."

She stepped toward him. Her look seemed out of proportion.

"I saw you checking from the hallway. That was important."

"I'm glad it's over," he said. "You handled it well. You were very gracious."

That night, he slept poorly. In the middle of a strange dream, Nagle walked toward him. She stopped and undressed.

"What's the difference now?" she said.

Lockett stayed awake, trying to remember, not trying to remember. Blurred boundaries unsettled him: the civility, the long legs, the love of poetry, and the same smile that looked like a kiss.

Until then, some days in class had been almost frightening. He knew he'd been winging it and so did the students, some sympathized, others simply wanted three credits. What he wasn't had taken too much time with this class. Little by little, his confidence grew after Nagle's remarks. By November, he had adjusted his cadence and lecture style. He revised lectures almost note by note until the order became more natural. He listened to his stories as if to learn for himself, relevant stories from Grand Lac, or the Navy, or graduate school, asking questions, laughing at bad jokes poached from old mentors.

"Why isn't poker played in the jungle?"

"Too many cheetahs."

"You heard the stadium got hot after the football game?"

"Fans left."

Students groaned. But they warmed to the change and responded to his questions.

Two weeks later, Nagle was slow to leave after class.

"You're having fun," she said, "you could be dangerous."

She put her head down.

"Something happened to me. Can I tell you about it?"

He hesitated. He knew he had grown fond of her since her compliment. Affection one way, responsibility another, "Yes" seemed like an excuse.

But he said, "Yes, please."

"At night, I feed logs to the fire. I study or write. In the summer, I walk naked in the woods. It's almost all aspen up there. I look to where the moon will be. In the winter, the light comes through without the leaves. Last night, I followed the same path in the snow. It reminded me of us, a little incomplete, a little physical. I know how you look at me during class. I wondered if we were cheating or being cheated. I wasn't afraid, but I cried. Being lost is sometimes the way I learn."

Lockett felt the quiver in his stomach.

"That's a compliment," he said. "I'm sorry if I make you nervous. I'm glad we're friends."

She grinned.

"Thank you. I told you, you're dangerous."

The first blizzard came through the weekend before Thanksgiving. Ten inches of snow and blowing drifts left uncovered wood piles frozen until spring. Saturday morning, Lockett walked a mile and half to the campus on unplowed streets.

An hour later, Damien Rice propped his boots on the corner of Lockett's desk looking like anything but third generation Boston Irish. He was dressed as usual with old cowboy boots, a blue chambray shirt and faded Levi's. Lockett thought about their first conversation when they were paired working freshman registration in September.

"Girl's get prettier every year," he had said.

"They're the same every September," Rice said, "only you're a year older."

That was the beginning with the unpredictable Yale anthropologist.

Rice had gone on to talk about how he handled his classes. He said he held test reviews in the grungiest bars he could find and told students to pick up some of the Spanish. He talked about a girl who told him she didn't like to read books.

"Can you imagine? We should be eager to give our judgements about what's worth reading and lead them to it. How the hell can you teach about relationships and art and music and culture without teaching them to read critically? Students end up believing fools. English teachers who can't diagram a sentence? Everything dumbed down."

He described how he broke horses each summer in Tucson.

"I enjoy it, no, I need it. I fit better with the cowboys. I get bored except for my students. My wife is from Radcliffe. I have a hard time explaining it to her. I'm sure it will happen here, faculty who've gone straight through, kindergarten to a Ph.D. They know their subject, that's all they know. Incredibly bland, never worked with their hands, built a house, no military, never in street fight, no time in a mine, or on a dock. Ever been to a party with faculty and lawyers? Metaphor for yawning. Lethal."

He paused.

"I've got an older student who's knocking the hell out of my curve. She's a professional stripper. She said she'd join me during the intermission at one of her shows. Can you imagine one of those guys sitting next to a stripper without his lecture notes? Sue's in California at her parents this weekend. Why not come along?"

Lockett laughed.

"Jesus, Rice, faculty sex symbol? Every father's nightmare, every coed's dream."

"What?" Rice said.

"You heard me. I read it somewhere. She's in my intro too, and you got the invitation?"

. "She probably knows you're not serious about women, Oliver. You make 'em too mysterious."

Lockett told him he might be right. Rice rolled his eyes.

"If clarity is what you want you should have been a monk. Well, maybe not..."

He paused.

"You ever read the Russians? Chekov said what's most important is not to lie to ourselves. When we do, we start listening to our own stuff, time comes when a man stops knowing how to love. I'm not talking about marriage, Oliver, I've done it twice, it's not so bad. They both had great taste in men. At least you can slow the process before you become an angry old man."

Lockett interrupted.

"I get that, Damien. You think marriage cures anything? It doesn't put anybody out of any misery. Expecting it to produce happiness is a little delusional. Some guys need a woman like a habit. I don't. Like knowing all you'll ever eat is pizza. I have a problem with that."

Rice leaned back with his hands behind his head.

"Everything that happens is a disappointment? The past shouldn't be your enemy, Oliver. Next you're going to tell me you're going to the Christmas Tea. Another drawbridge to cross? Go ahead, you can tell me."'

He grinned.

"Did I tell you? She said sorority girls have odds on which of you they bed first, you or some guy in chemistry named Barrett. He's even money by the end of the school year. You're a lot higher. Even the girls figure you'll be tougher. Faculty aren't the only ones who collect pelts."

Lockett pulled in a breath and changed the subject.

"Watch your ass, Damien. You might as well be in some foreign port as a place like that. Strip clubs, open sewage, and every sailor in every joint thinks some stripper wants him. World could come to an end with those cowboys."

Rice laughed. The conversation ran another five minutes before Lockett began leafing through a stack of papers. Rice read the hint. He swung his legs off the desk and walked toward the door.

"You're starting to walk funny, Damien. Too many horses? Joints need oiling?"

Rice opened the door and turned.

"My joints need oiling? My joints? You're gonna tell me about that? You're a case study, man. What keeps you going?"

Lockett laughed.

"There's a rumor that Chekov lacked an appetite for sex."

Rice closed the door.

Lockett stood and looked at snow covering everything into the mountains. Young Mrs. King had been a sorority girl.

But Rice had been at least partly right. Lockett had friends, good friends. And there were times he enjoyed himself. He understood the almost cruel way he had crawled out a bed and promised to call. And the evenings, like the Mansion in Dallas, the pretty dark haired woman in the loose white blouse with breasts that probably weren't hers, in so much pain she couldn't hear herself.

"We built houses in South Lake and Highland Park. He built them. I decorated them. He never cared about much except I get real wet. I got excited and real wet."

She finished the mojito and turned.

"You want to see the rest of 'em, don't you. I know you do." She was putting in too much effort. And the plastic said as much about her mind as her body.

He rested his elbows on the bar and looked at the mirror. She was pretty, probably orgasms like Dairy Queens, but not enough to listen to the same thing again in the morning.

She knew his answer. She looked sad.

"I guess I'm not your girlfriend tonight."

Lockett took a deep breath.

"No, I wish you were, but you're not."

He'd never thought about it before, how a man could marry a pretty artificial hybrid so fucked up with anger that she might become his ex wife and never talk to him again.

He remembered, a little over a year earlier, the Times Picayune article by the Houston food editor who claimed he had found the best gumbo in New Orleans. At six o'clock, Lockett took a cab to an unpainted shotgun shack in the ninth ward. The sign said Beverot's. A small blackboard hung lopsided next to the door and listed the menu in colored chalk. Two older black men shot eight ball in a room to the left. A light skinned Creole waitress smiled and told him to sit anywhere. He ordered a Budweiser.

143

A minute later, an old black man with a neat white beard came from somewhere in the back. He pulled a chair from another table. He introduced himself as Lonzo Beverot. He told how his father started the restaurant with lunches, and how the place became a gathering spot after the war. Lonzo remembered talking to the editor from Houston.

"That's the business in New Orleans," he said, "restaurants come and go. The article won't change anything here."

He hoped Lockett would enjoy his supper and thanked him for coming. They shook and he left.

Lockett ordered a bowl of seafood gumbo. Almost as if planned, a tall woman entered in a grey A line dress that hid her figure. Early crows feet made her more attractive. They exchanged glances. He stood and she offered her hand.

"I'm Madeline Norris. Do you mind if I join you?"

She was poised, the kind of charm that came from a good southern girl's school.

A moment later, Lonzo returned. He hugged her and they chatted. After he left, she ordered gumbo and said she visited at least once a year. New Orleans was where she met her husband a decade earlier. She described a hard working surgeon in Atlanta who she put through medical school with a trust fund. He loved his work but not travel. Beverot's had been their favorite place outside the French Quarter.

"I need new experiences," she said, "so I come here alone. Even if I don't have the time, I travel. I feed my eyes and my soul. I find satisfaction."

Lockett lifted his chin as if trying to think ahead. He had been fascinated by two or three women the governor had called "trust funds and regrets," before he stopped dating them.

As they ate, they traded small talk about the city, the mix of New Orleans cultures, favorite restaurants, and avoiding Mardi Gras.

"There's a dream quality about being here," she said. "I love my husband, but I want to experience more."

An hour later they ordered Muscat at the Windsor Court.

"It's purely instinctive," she said. "I let things happen, then I go back. There are certain times to do certain things. I try not to judge it. It works out alright."

They undressed with his balcony doors open. She smiled as she watched him look.

"If you can't use your body to accomplish something good," she said, "it's just an ornament."

In the morning, they drank coffee on the balcony.

"Sometimes it's like the Mississippi," she said, "it's best with no boundaries. To me, that's what makes evenings like last night worth it."

Her eyes filled with tears. She shook her head.

"How did I end up with a husband?"

She left a few minutes later. Lockett stayed on the humid balcony breathing her perfume. He smiled at her idea of a body as more than an ornament. This time it just happened to be with him. He wondered how she ended up with a husband.

A hard winter came every day through mid December. Blizzards closed interstates. Ski resorts shut down twice.

145

Two Navajo men died walking on the reservation until they got too cold. Fifty five mile an hour wind gusts blew snow that fell at four inches an hour, enough to rank near the top of the snowiest days in a century.

Murch arrived early the Monday before Christmas vacation. He asked if he could speak to the class. Lockett hesitated. He had done about as much as he wanted to with him. He had no interest in turning him loose this late in the semester.

"What's it about, Clyde?"

Murch described a mother and two young children he picked up over the weekend during another storm.

"Nightgown, pajamas, no jackets. I took them to a foster place we use. They're there now. They're alright. But it's not going to be much of a Christmas. I thought the class might chip in and buy food and maybe a couple of gifts, at least for the kids. I'd like to collect a dollar a piece."

Collecting money from a class was probably against university rules, but Lockett liked the idea. Twenty one students, Murch wouldn't get them all but some might give more.

Murch was calm with his story. He suggested a dollar and said he'd get sizes and details for Wednesday. They could figure when to shop and a night for Santa, maybe Thursday. Roe offered the small tree from her room and included the lights and decorations. Anna Kewanemtewa said she was going home to the reservation, she wouldn't need her wreath. Classmates volunteered for the supermarket: bread, peanut butter, canned ham, rice, breakfast cereal. By the time he finished, he had touched them all.

Kofman approached while Murch collected the money.

"I'll make up whatever we need to make sure the kids get good clothes."

Murch asked for a copy of the class roster. By Wednesday, he had talked to everyone and checked with the old foster couple.

"Most planned to leave tomorrow morning," he said, "but they want to help, and be there when Santa comes. The foster couple is fine with Thursday. It's best to shop this afternoon and then wrap."

It was the first time Lockett saw Murch smile.

Thursday night, fireplace smoke filled the air in the middle of a string of unlighted blocks with mid century ranch houses decorated in red, green and white holiday lights. Cyclone fences controlled barking dogs. Students mingled and laughed in the front yard of the gray bungalow whose paint had peeled away from years of mountain winds. Lockett sensed the difference since September. In some ways, the semester had been a bigger problem than he could have ever imagined. But he had adjusted, the classroom had changed and students were celebrating.

He stood near the back in his Navy foul weather jacket with a black Irish wool scarf. Nagle approached in a white ski jacket and tight black ski pants. She bumped his hip and grinned. Lockett remembered snow, and cold, and another Christmas, how young he had been with Molly, and again tonight, how delightful things could be when someone special cared with you. Maybe Rice was right about the past as an enemy. Maybe he shouldn't regret this time the same way.

147

Nearby, Poe held hands with her boyfriend, a tall blond surfer from Huntington Beach, and the school's quarterback. As they walked past, he whispered, "Cute ass." Nagle ignored it, as if it wasn't the first time she had been told about a body that made boys restless. Casey looked comfortable with Garcia's left arm around her neck cupping a breast near the door.

Santa lead into Jingle Bells. The old couple opened the door. Students entered the light with arms full of grocery bags and Christmas packages. The little boy's eyes got big as he reached for his mother's hand. A little girl, four or five, slid off the couch and locked on to Santa's leg. Murch picked her up and hugged her. Kewanemptewa balanced on Kofman's shoulders to tack her wreath high above the door. Dowd worked with Poe and her boyfriend to set the tree with lights in a corner near the window. The young mother began to cry.

Nagle slipped her hand into Lockett's pocket.

"Aren't you cold?" she said.

Her fingers closed the space between them. Lockett angled his body toward her, the same protective sense he had during the incident with Kofman. She turned her face up.

"It's different isn't it. Have we settled?"

She reached and brushed her fingertips against his face.

"Sometimes we make love without touching. Sometimes, when I find myself with that person, it's just a touch. That kind of lovemaking, the special kind, it comes back."

Lockett lifted his chin. It didn't seem crazy to be at peace with whatever it was and how good it might be.

Some things you stayed with. Maybe one day they re-solved themselves. Or you destroy yourself.

Ruthie Murch's hair had been dyed a darker shade to enforce the original red. She bubbled over as she approached talking about taking charge of eleven girls and seven boys shopping at Hansen's supermarket and Sear's.

"I can't tell you how much fun I had with those kids," she said. "Just nice kids. You'd love the clothes, so cute, so practical. Snow pants, mittens, pajamas. And toys, a truck, a beautiful doll, games they can play together."

She talked about how happy her husband was. She told how they met in Phoenix, how one of his first arrests was in a battered baby case, how he took vacation to stay with the little girl in the hospital.

"I'm an ER nurse. The baby died and he's never gotten over it. He's like that with every kid. We can't have children. But he's a fine husband and a good cop."

She looked around, away from the doorway. She hid her smile with a large green mitten.

"And I didn't see a thing. Nobody noticed, and I didn't see a thing, I promise."

She gripped Lockett's hand.

"Time for me to catch up with Santa."

Nagle watched her walk away. She tipped her head as if thinking.

"If you spend any time in the mountains, especially in winter, it's hard to think of yourself as very important. Last night I climbed an old summer trail. I imagined our tracks in the snow together. When I got back to the cabin, I had a glass of wine and thought about dancing nude with you. Sex and poetry have always been rewards for me. I

149

masturbated in front of the fireplace. Then I started a poem."

She pulled a small tablet from her jacket pocket and flipped to a back page.

"Go ahead," she said, "please, read it out loud."

> I have watched him for weeks,
> Alongside him like a lover,
> Breathing the air he is exhaling,
> Hiding my free fall from him.
> We are comrades not calling out,
> Pretending all is well.

She paused, for a long time.

"If the gift is taken away, we still manage to keep the meaning."

Lockett watched snowflakes fly into new drifts. He thought about the smiling eyes that seemed to insist on something more those first weeks, that not everything was decaying faster than he could follow.

Nagle shuffled her boots.

"We're not insane. We're not monsters. You shielded me when I needed it. It's a good chemistry. It could happen to anyone."

She looked down and grinned.

"But you never tried to seduce me. I'm not sure I'm happy about that."

A minute later, she started a sentence.

"I have to…"

She paused.

"I have to catch up with some friends."

The wind picked up spinning more snow. They walked to the corner. As if for a last time, they held each other and kissed.

"We both have places to go," she said.

She crossed the street. He watched her look back before she joined a group headed into the next block without street lights.

The next morning, Eden raised his hand.

"Love is when someone gives birth and falls in love with her obstetrician."

Happ followed.

"What do you get when you decorate at Christmas?"

"Tinselitis," somebody said.

The class hissed. Lockett grinned at what he had created.

Eden suggested that the class thank Murch. Students clapped. Lockett traded his planned lecture for a comment about the night before.

"Gratitude is an active response to something we've been given. Sometimes it's as simple as a classroom. Sometimes it's like what happened last night, the relationship between individuals and the larger society. At its best, it's thankfulness."

He moved to the door and wished students a Merry Christmas as they left. Nagle was the last to leave.

"We should be grateful for our classrooms," she said, "they can be the difference."

Lockett grinned.

"You're dangerous, you know."

A few seconds passed before her last smile.

Murch returned a minute later like he'd forgotten something.

"We're not done yet," he said. "If you still want to ride, I'll pick you up around four."

Lockett thought about the irony, a semester of aggravation from the same student who had enriched his life last night. The least he could do was ride.

That afternoon, they drove three miles past old tourist courts before Murch left route sixty six. He went another three blocks to a parking lot with six rundown motel units from the forties. He hammered the office door with the side of his fist.

"Herrera," he hollered.

A middle-aged Hispanic opened the door in an undershirt stained with what looked like guacamole. His stomach stood out in every direction. His right eye was covered with a black patch as menacing as the old brown buildings. His hands were scraped with patches of skin missing from his knuckles. Lockett imagined a fight gone bad. It was obvious he had met Murch.

"What do you want?"

"We want to talk about number five, the couple with two kids. First, I want a look. The keys."

"You been there, nothing wrong."

He closed the door halfway before Murch put a foot out to stop it.

"Goddammit," Herrera said, "it's cold."

"The keys, Oscar. Just give me the keys. Now."

Number five smelled like cigarillos mixed with urine. The space had two slatted chairs, an unmade Murphy bed, and a drop down table that hooked to a nail on the wall. A small 1940's refrigerator and a two coil electric cooktop were plugged into the same receptacle.

"They all slept in one bed. Look at this."

Murch opened the refrigerator. The inside was warm and smelled like spoiled milk. On the shelves were a rotting tomato, two taco shells and two cans of Schlitz.

Three minutes later, they knocked on the office door again. Herrera held a Dos Equis and a cigarette.

"Told you, nothing wrong."

"How much do you get for it, the room, monthly?"

"Goes by the week, twenty five. You done?"

Murch stared.

"The mother and the kids are coming back after Christmas, a month, maybe longer. Place needs a refrigerator, a new mattress, and another bed. Two beds, Oscar, not worth twenty five. From now on it's ten, ten a week as long as they stay."

Herrera clinched his jaw.

"You can't do that, I'm outside the city limits."

Murch's expression didn't change.

"Just did, amigo, don't test it. You want the county? I'll bring the sheriff."

Herrera's face turned red. He jabbed a finger.

"You son of a bitch."

Until then, Murch had been calm. He pushed his tongue in his cheek and inhaled.

"You still running that poker game with your fat friends, Oscar? Saturday nights? Sure you are. It's rigged. Lose that game and you lose a lot more than fifteen bucks a week. The rent's ten, make up the difference from the suckers you play with. Otherwise the sheriff stops with his own warrant. We'll shut the whole place down, see how that feels."

He cleared his throat.

"Fix the damned unit, Herrera. Don't screw it up. I'll be checking every day. Tough to run a game from behind bars."

"Fuck you," Herrera said. Spit flew from his mouth. Murch squared his shoulders.

"Be careful wetback. Anything goes wrong, you'll regret the day your whore mother hatched you under that rock. You'll die too poor to buy underwear for your sorry ass, even in Merido."

Lockett thought about the classroom, how Murch believed that men like Herrera were born evil because of what happened to the children, something that wouldn't be corrected by the legal system.

Mountain winds pushed cold air as they walked to their car.

"That's how real justice works," Murch said. "It's not something I just came up with. Did I tell you? We put the husband on a bus back to Texas. Told him what would happen if we ever saw him again. He's been beating her for years. We'll get her a job, help with the kids. He won't be back."

He settled in the driver's seat and checked himself in the mirror. He looked at Lockett.

"You learn a lot about a man when you catch him in his own world, doc. When you have to fix a place for kids in it, that's when you know he's from hell."

Lockett knew there were evil people who were blind to consequences, or rejected right answers about their behavior. Some felt their anger but chose to be virtuous about it. The real problem was the suffering they brought to others by avoiding the right choice. Lucque had said if we admit that anything can be more important than love, we can justify any crime. Lockett couldn't remember anybody as evil and indifferent as Herrera.

Murch believed differently, that Herrera was born that way because of what he had done to the kids. That was his choice. But this was not the place for a lecture.

Murch grinned like he knew more.

"I'm glad you came along, doc. Like you said, somethings save more than they cost."

Lockett's thoughts scattered.

"Have you ever imagined there are answers you don't have, Clyde, there are some things you don't know?"

Murch frowned and blinked.

Lockett pressed his lips to hide a smile.

"You know what a seven-course Cajun breakfast is?"

Murch gave a nervous laugh.

"No," he said.

"A pound of boudin and a six pack."

Time would leap forward and the Thursday night would be more and more difficult to forget and the day would come once a year when Lockett would remember the shine in her eyes and hear her voice and remember her words and feel her arms and taste her kiss and wonder where she was and he would grow and be comfortable with all of it as part of some larger purpose both too much and too little that got it right even that much.

But it's not the kind of story you should tell everyone.

AS IF A REVISION WOULD BE IN ORDER

"And what rough beast, its time come round at last,
Slouches toward Bethlehem to be born."

W. B. Yeats, *The Second Coming*

When the cab passed through the gate, Lockett thought the place looked lovely, but he'd bet it wasn't. Worse yet was the idea that he'd be there in place of the Ninth Circle people he'd left behind.

That spring, the Mississippi ran high and fast. A month earlier, he started a conversation with his doctor about jogging on the levee. They talked about the unusual number of hummingbirds that died on the *batture* that spring after migrating from Central America. They agreed, a smile on the levee made everyone feel a little more cheerful.

"Just simple southern courtesies," Sublette said. "You've been here long enough, you've seen it. The whole world becomes more civil. So do the coeds, a menagerie, the bodies, you know. Some, you smell the perfume…"

Lockett didn't answer but he wasn't surprised. Sublette had a reputation as a fool for a looker. This was probably not his first fantasy about his daughter's sorority sisters. And, like he said, he had seen them, the shapely ones with pretty smiles, and the sad ones who looked like they wanted to ask if something would ever be over, as if they couldn't hold it together for another day.

Sublette asked about the chest pains. Lockett said he wasn't sure. He told about pain in his right side when he jogged the week before, and how it came back the next day, pushing wrought iron furniture around his patio.

Sublette raised an eyebrow. He asked about breathing, and anything since. Lockett said no, but he hadn't done anything since. Sublette said he'd schedule an angiogram for the afternoon. He put his hand on Lockett's shoulder. He began the usual questions: exercise, sleep, diet, and the one about alcohol. Lockett told him a couple of beers.

"Every day?"

"Just about."

Late that afternoon, the angiogram showed a small blockage. Sublette called it stress. He said the blockage was too small for a stent, Lockett's heart could handle it, and he should keep running.

"Good for the endorphins."

He prescribed Prozac and warned against mixing it with alcohol.

A week later, a combination of rainy days, sleepless nights and toxic hangovers gave Lockett the perfect excuse to quit running. Drinking seemed to help everything, except for Chinese gongs in his head the next morning, and hopelessness like the girls on the levee.

Creative Alternatives called itself "a place for awareness and healing, your best chance to be wary of who you are."

Lockett was assigned a private room, basically a monk's cell with white walls, no carpet, no television, an open closet and a double bed with a navy blue wool blanket at the foot. A small book case was empty except for a copy of *The Big Book*. He smiled at the question he had heard about whether people went to A.A. meetings because they believed in A.A. or they believed because they went. Alcoholic seemed like such a loaded word.

Around five the next morning, he opened the window about three inches. It had been a long time since he inhaled fresh rain mixed with wild grass and fir. A fading moon showed the shadow of an abandoned barn a half mile away. Ten yards out, a healthy looking white cat sat patiently watching a yellow male finch focused on a mate. In another month, the rest should all look green like the color of hope. Maybe his luck would change like the morning he first saw Molly.

He pulled on tan shorts, a black Polo and Ecco sandals. The hallway was empty, except to the left of his door where he surprised a red headed woman dozing on a white upholstered folding chair with a *Time* magazine on her lap. She looked like his former secretary who got measured by men the way only red heads get measured. She blinked, as surprised to see him as he was to see her. Her ID badge read Emma Reed, Counselor. She stood and extended her hand.

"Good morning," she said.

Lockett said good morning, unsure about where to go after that. It didn't matter. He had come to Topeka thinking rehab might as well be a place to die. But you're not supposed to die when you are fifty-eight. Like a lot of what he couldn't control, he had become ashamed of his worthlessness and uncertain about a future to erase the past.

"Face it," his ex wife had said, "you're a bum, just like your father."

He wondered how many of the thirty days would be crazy and how many would be real, or if he would ever know. Maybe it wouldn't be until it was all over that he'd learn whether "one day at a time" was more than just a cliche. He was tired of thinking of himself as the victim. For now, he'd trade the time for what the place claimed. Or at least some clarity.

What the hell, thirty days, maybe one day he'd remember it as a lucky escape. After what it took to get there, it was almost nice to not be alone.

When he checked in, Lockett heard, "Greetings, you will recover or die." Nobody said it, but that's what it sounded like. That was before they scolded him for mixing Prozac with Absolut, and Beck's, and Clos du Bois Marlestone.

"Four beers, three martinis, a half bottle of wine? Every day? That could have killed you. Didn't your doctor warn you?"

"He never knew," Lockett said.

Anyway, Hemingway and Carver said booze took a long time if you got good at it.

He assumed they kept him on the Prozac to help with answers that hadn't been close during the year after he lost his job and his wife moved to her new bosses' cabin.

The patient's job, they said, was to "dig deeper for a signal that will pull you out and get your life back together."

That was the dream and the attraction, the beginning of something, just that he wasn't sure what.

"Ms. Reed," he said, "surely you're not here to watch me go through the DT's."

Reed seemed like midwestern women who survived smoke filled bars and left the impression they could survive on any masculine island. She patted him on the arm.

"It's a standard precaution for all new patients. We'll talk more about it at the morning meeting."

Lockett swallowed hard. A Band Aid answer like the DT's to figure out his world was as silly as it was absurd.

She picked up her chair and paused.

"You had reason for optimism once, Oliver. Hope is a vision for the future. You don't survive despite your failures, you survive because of your failures. That's what feeds hope, room for imagination, for what's possible. There is honor in replacing one hope with another."

She finished. And he was out of conversation. He followed her until she passed the kitchen. He was sure that in an hour, enough characters to populate a neighborhood would trace the smell of coffee.

The first week, Lockett slept peacefully, six straight mornings without a hangover and three Tylenol. He listened at Alcoholics Anonymous meetings that said he was no different than the others on board what the depressed gay druggist from Duluth called their "cargo ship for ambiguity:" addicts, problem drinkers, chronic drinkers, high functioning alcoholics. Meetings were filled with confessions and tears. What anybody said seemed more important than what somebody else said. Almost everyone trotted out something called "character flaws" like ailments or infections. The most religious seemed comfortable with the word "surrender." If the A.A. medical model with religious solutions didn't hold, well, that was the patient's fault.

At ten grand down and twelve hundred a day, patients were hardly drunks leaning up against vacant buildings. Some needed comfort, others needed audiences. All seemed wrapped up in fantasies about love, money or who they were. Most had traveled to unimaginable places, losing families, reputations, fortunes, struggling with anger, guilt, shame and depression. Twenty two strangers, re-structuring stories from fragile childhoods to open sex, looking for whatever they could get from understanding, support and approval.

For Lockett it was about cowardice, satisfying what he knew, and what he didn't.

Ten days later, his voice quivered before he confessed he had lost his courage. He broke down and cried.

"I'm afraid to disappoint anyone any more."

Emma patted him on the back, like calming a baby.

"No, you've lost your confidence. The nice thing is that you'll get the chance to prove yourself again. You'll find a job, away from the pricey clutter and pretension you left."

She paused.

"There is a language of love, Oliver. It's just not in bed, it's every day in what we say and how we say it. That's real intimacy. That's what translates to the bed. One day a woman will touch your face and tell you she loves you. Believe her."

By mid June, thirty days had lined up to make rehab worth it. His mind had become clearer.

Exchanges with his psychiatrist had been blunt.

"You're right, Oliver, you're right again. You're a smart guy, and nobody gives a shit. Nobody wants elo-quence. It's not about being smarter than the next guy. Is that the mountain you want to die on? Being smart? Life is not about the dead vanity of knowing better, Oliver. What I want is your secret."

Thursday of the fourth week, Lockett visited Dr. Sam Madoff for the last time. The door was open. The psychiatrist listened on the phone and jotted something on a legal pad. He raised his arm and pointed to a chair.

Late afternoon light filled the paneled office. French windows opened to graveled paths beside beds of giant sun flowers. A dozen acres had changed to green. Lockett remembered Keats' new hope: "The stubble plain looks warm."

Books filled shelves from the floor to the ceiling, nothing alphabetical, nothing by subject or author. And not just on shelves. A leather bound collection of Dostoevsky, Tolstoy and Chekhov sat on a Persian rug next to six or eight other books. Small piles covered a chair and a window sill. On the floor, collections of poetry and renderings by Rumi, Hafez, Rilke, and Kabir stacked up next to Madoff's desk.

"I like books," Madoff said in their first meeting. "I like having them close. They're spiritual supports. They make my life work. It's reassuring. I think I learn most from Chekhov."

Lockett sat in a whiskey colored leather club chair, alongside a brass end table with a glass top and a paperback called *Daily Reminders*. He paged back to his birthday: "It's not the load that breaks down. It's the way you carry it."

Madoff hung up the phone and glanced at his computer. He turned and folded his arms. Lockett set the book on the table.

"We need to hear voices like that," Madoff said, "anything we can do to get some ideas about staying well. Take it. I've got another copy."

Lockett said thank you.

Madoff wouldn't waste a good book on someone he didn't have confidence in even if he had two copies. The book was a compliment.

Madoff turned on his desk lamp. He told Lockett he would be released in the morning. He warned about patients who left as if they were starting a book they would revise and revise and hope that the next version would be perfect.

"Bonhoffer called it a cheap grace," he said, "the notion of feeling good while avoiding difficult responsibilities."

He told him that no matter what he did, he shouldn't do that. He said he would be uncomfortable for a while.

"That's what happens when we let go. It's not like shedding old skin. It's treating the past like a fossil. You preserve, you study and learn. You said your ex-wife's lover threatened to kill you? That should tell you something about the people you left behind."

"My attorney told me he had a reputation for money and a small penis."

Madoff paused.

"That's exactly what I'm talking about, Oliver, the kind of thought you leave behind. We're all a river. We go through things on the surface or deep. We have a soul but we pay too much attention to comparing and looking good. That's the surface they'll be remembered for, not their soul. They can't stop the river."

He paused.

"They'll say you were a part of it and they'll be right. You compared as much as they did, car, house, the need to believe that everyone else was equally unreal. Louisiana should be a sleeping dog to you now. Leave it that way. Pay attention to what this experience tells you, otherwise, you're headed back to the same sickness."

Madoff looked again at the tablet. He wrote something. He underlined it and folded his arms. He stared past Lockett like Lucque when he was thinking.

"And one last question. Early in your stay, you mentioned a young woman named Molly. I'm curious. Is that another secret? Tell me the story, how you met, a little about what she meant."

WHAT HAPPENS AFTER THE WORDS RUN OUT

"Not a day goes by,
Not a single day,
But you're somewhere a part of my life
And it looks like you'll stay...
George S. Kaufman, Moss Hart, *Merrily We Roll Along*

Lockett had trusted Madoff during the most vulnerable days in his life.

"I lost her," he said. "It's complicated. It covers a lot of ground."

Madoff leaned forward. He pointed to the leather-bound collection on the shelf.

"Everyone can understand falling in love and losing that person. Dostoyevsky said man has no more anxiety than to find someone he worships. And you never found her again?"

Lockett told about the early days, the first time Clear mentioned Molly, about the September morning on the way to school, and the night on the VFW stairs. He described the early days and the letters she wrote during the Navy. After he got out, people seemed confused about where she had gone. They said, with her looks, she went anywhere she wanted. But this time her looks had gotten in the way of what she knew was important.

"And you haven't seen her since the 1958 Christmas?"

Lockett replayed much of what he said earlier about his divorce, what he had called the smell of a burn ward.

Madoff interrupted.

"Vomiting at work doesn't mean you're bad at your job."

Lockett didn't answer. He talked about the two years, trying to fill another space between sunrise and sunset after his divorce, what the French called *anomie*. He had made up his mind to travel, something fresh, a few days somewhere else. A conference at St. Mary's University in San Antonio that April seemed perfect. The meeting brochure recommended a dozen places to eat: "Our good restaurants lead with their senses."

During the first morning break, he called for a reservation at a place recommended by the St. Mary's dean.

At five thirty, the restaurant was alive in a way few things had been for a long time. Waiters smiled as they passed each other in semi formal black suits and bow ties. A dark haired hostess with a pixie cut and a discrete black cocktail dress stood alongside an attractive maitre'd in a fitted black suit with a v neck. Lockett thought about the conference material: "Good restaurants lead with their senses."

The maitre'd stood straight and quiet. Her wide mouth was the kind women disagreed with but most men thought was attractive. She stared. She took a step, shoulders back, chest out, chin up. They grinned, like a hundred times before.

"It's really you," Molly said.

They hugged, not long, but not caring what anyone thought.

"It's been a while," he said.

She smiled.

"I saw your name in the book. I never thought it would be you."

She stepped back.

"I always pictured you in a charcoal suit."

She was still pretty in a way women weren't pretty any more. Her pale honey hair was swept left with bangs that emphasized her eyes. They talked through the noise of early reservations. She seated him in the middle of the room and sat for two minutes.

"Look at me," she said, "let me know you're really here."

Forty five minutes later he finished the tiramisu and folded his napkin. She walked to his table. She seated herself and whispered.

"You either feel these things or you don't. Can you come back? I'll close early."

Adrenaline charged Lockett's brain, like remembering a beautiful dream.

His heart jumped.

"I'll be back."

In his room he stretched out on the bed. He felt shamelessly happy. He recalled fragments, like Sister Cecelia's words that seemed so meaningless at the time: "You find happiness with people you can count on, then you have to hold on to it. You may not find it in the way you expect."

Maybe people never knew how much they meant to each other until something like this happened. If God punishes him, he will give him tonight and say something like, "One night is all the complete happiness you can ever expect from me."

The hours dragged like a long movie. Just after ten, Molly opened a bottle of 1974 Stag's Leap cabernet. Lockett had imagined it a hundred times, not the wine, not the accident, but the chance again.

For almost four hours they became each other's audience, as eager as they had ever been, trying to fit in everything like the first night on the stairs. Some details had faded, others had become clearer: small talk about old street lights and how quiet it got when they came on, details about the jackets they carried each summer when a cold wind could switch from the lake at any time, and the smell of burning leaves in the fall.

They laughed at the Sunday afternoon they got caught in a downpour and pressed against the brownstones on twenty first to keep dry. They remembered getting wet anyway and holding hands and skipping four blocks to her house "like third graders." She recalled the night they hid from a sprinkle of rain eating chocolate peanut butter cups under a red awning in front of the electric shop on Belknap.

"We kissed on that busy street," she said. "I didn't mind but my folks would have died."

Lockett told her about the games he played after the Navy.

"You had moved. Your friends said, 'you know Molly, she lives her life on what drives her.' I thought if I could find your college I could sit down in the middle of the campus and you'd come by."

"The trick for me was to enjoy the memories," she said. "There was so much. I put the past behind a wall. But behind the wall was a garden. And it was always in bloom. I taught myself to not want more than what had been. But I still wanted to see blooms behind the wall."

She remembered each of his birthdays. And waking after a blizzard, when schools were closed, when they talked as long as they could on the phone. She asked if he remembered their first Christmas and the Rosetti poem. She touched his face.

"Well I never got fat."

"That was the first time we hugged," he said. "I remember the kiss and thinking Christmas came early."

She smiled.

"You don't wear a ring."

He told her about why he was in San Antonio.

"In the end, we both failed the marriage. Later I realized that wasn't all of it."

She squeezed his hand, the same reassurance she had shown dozens of times decades earlier.

"And you?" he said.

She parted her lips. They had married without ever really knowing each other.

"It was part of running. He was older. I thought he was more mature. He golfed. My mother loved that. I watched the way guys sneaked looks at tournaments. It's another way they compete, trophy dates, trophy wives. I let myself be a decoration."

She flipped her hair back.

"The counselor said some men live inside a woman like another prize. She called it borrowing an ego. One person wants to stay together, so they think the other person still loves them. It was costing us. I started working five years ago."

She cleared her throat.

"I've had other lovers. I used them to let me know more about myself. I've never had a notion of a life without you.'

She sat back. She remembered what people said after he left for the Navy.

"They said I'd get over it, that I'd be happy again."

One friend called her besotted. When another one asked when she had stopped crying she told her she hadn't.

She spread three wallet sized pictures of her daughter on the table.

"She's my best friend."

The girl looked like Molly at seventeen. Lockett touched each picture, as if contact made the girl closer.

He asked about her work.

She said it made her happy in a way she hardly thought of as work. Her customers were "reserved." They knew good conversation and manners and the difference between eating and dining.

"Dealing with good taste can be very liberating. I'd almost forgotten about how happy people can be."

She took a sip of wine. She talked about her plans for nursing school.

He told her about Flagstaff and the years since. Her eyes danced at the story about Amanda, as if she could imagine how it happened.

She leaned in.

"I almost forgot. Clear? Do you ever see him?"

Lockett touched her hand. He heard his voice go flat.

"He died in nineteen sixty one."

They had ended up at the Texaco station that morning. Clear was with McVitie, Fitz, and another guy he worked with. They hoped it was warmer at Nebagamon to water ski. He was driving a new convertible he had bought for Jackie.

"I don't think it was his idea. The others wanted me to come with them. Clear didn't seem excited. That was a Sunday. It was September and I told them I had a history test in the morning. The new guy danced around my car calling me a smart college boy. Clear pulled alongside before they left. He rolled down his window. He looked down and shook his head about something."

Lockett paused.

"They missed a turn that night. Clear was the only one killed. Nobody knows who was driving. The others never said. Nobody thought it was Clear. The whole thing seemed unfair."

Molly's shoulders dropped. She lowered her head.

"I'm trying to find the words but I can't," she said.

"He was always so nice."

Tears rolled down her face.

Lockett thought, maybe that's the way it is when somebody we love dies. You can't find the words.

"I never told you," she said. "I promised him I wouldn't. But he told me you were right behind him that night we met at the dance."

She smiled.

"That's how I ended up on those stairs."

Lockett grinned.

"It started with you," he said. "He liked you. He knew I'd like you. It was at a time when nothing else made sense for me. He just knew. But he didn't understand what was happening to me because I didn't understand. Things were happening around me and I responded, but I didn't understand."

Sometime after one, they finished the wine. He put his hand around her waist and she moved against him as they walked to the entrance. She said she was free until supper the next day and asked about his schedule. He agreed to skip the afternoon meetings. They kissed as if they had never been apart.

Before he fell asleep, he remembered Lucque's thirty year old words: "Love doesn't put you anywhere except to walk through whatever mysteries might be ahead."

Before daybreak, he jogged a three mile route along the river. A mile out, two figures appeared just as the sun rose. Seconds later, Willie Nelson raised his left hand for a high five.

"Hey man," he said.

His bodyguard nodded.

It would be a good day.

At noon, the air was filled with the scent of jalapeños.

They began where they had left off. Even disappointments seemed warm. She told how she kept his Navy letters in her dad's books.

"I didn't want to forget our stories or your handwriting."

They agreed, nobody could open themselves the way they had and not be hurt when it was gone.

For six months, they exchanged phone calls and long letters. They met again in September. The Anatole lobby in Dallas smelled of fresh roses on every table.

That night, Molly blushed as she removed the sheer Band Aids from her nipples.

"I don't usually suffer from vanity. Are you nervous?"

"A little," he said. "I'm happy."

An hour later she propped her face in her hands.

"My body was never a stranger to you. For years, all I've gotten from being touched was satisfaction from being wanted. I made sense of making love from memories." She paused, "At last."

She paused again.

"The night you came to the restaurant you said there was more to your divorce. Tell me about what she was like, your wife."

Lockett smiled.

"Do you remember *Breakfast at Tiffany's?* Where Tiffany's made her feel like nothing bad could happen? Our life wasn't Tiffany's. I had a good job that got us what we thought we needed. But we spent a lot of time training people to see us like we were at Tiffany's, putting a dollar sign on everything. She asked me once, toward the end, when I said I wanted to go back to teaching, if that was all I wanted to do, to teach."

Molly hooked his ankle with her foot and pulled him closer.

"One of my customers said the beauty of a puppy is that it lives in the present."

In the morning he smelled the scent of roses and warm sheets. They made love until noon and ate lunch at a cheap restaurant near the tennis courts. She rested her wine glass on her lap.

"I'm glad you're here. I want to live my life with that same feeling again, to go back and walk the streets, coming home, like the robin that morning. The birch trees on the lake are turning about now."

It was as if they knew, a home together defined more than a place.

That night, they showered until it all smelled like melons.

He told her he was confusing what melons and berries tasted like.

"Warm raspberries again?" she said.

"I like the thought," he said.

He sucked her nipples with an ice cube in his mouth. He imagined the wetness before she welcomed him into her.

Sunday morning they played in bed. They listened to what sounded like happy bells from a church somewhere in the neighborhood. They planned another visit, maybe San Antonio again, maybe New Orleans, longer the next time.

At mid afternoon, her voice cracked when her plane was called. They kissed with her hands on his face.

"I'll miss you. I love you."

Lockett took a dozen steps.

He turned and called.

"Hey!"

She looked back.

"I just wanted another look."

He sat down next to an old man with a cane and horn rimmed glasses. They watched her walk to the gate.

"I wish she'd come back," Lockett said.

The old man removed his glasses.

"Lord, don't we all."

She wrote a week later. Two weeks passed. It was nearly a month when she apologized for not responding to his letters.

"I'm embarrassed," she wrote.

Lockett wasn't prepared for her letter the day before Thanksgiving.

"Dear Oliver,
Thank you for returning, for taking me and my love again. I have learned what we have done for each other and what it means. I needed you as much as you needed me. Now I think I need you more. I am your life as much as you are mine, Oliver, but there are things that connect to bigger than ourselves. You have given me enough. The world will keep turning. I won't say goodby.
All my love,
Molly."

He pressed his fists into his forehead. He reread the letter. He could hear her words, the sounds of a missing child. How could it be? It wasn't fucking fair.

After that, he spent weeks deciding how much had been real. Maybe if they had spent more time together they could laugh or shrug and go on. Maybe "bigger than ourselves" was her marriage, but that could be temporary. Maybe he had looked for too much. But that's not what she said. Maybe the truth was that just finding her again should have been enough.

For months, he felt her thigh against him early in the morning. Outside, almost everything had died.

The move next spring wasn't all about her. But it was impossible to know what was truly happening. It could have been about her when he thought about losing all sense of what he knew and who he was. He imagined a house of mirrors, banging into parts that reflected, dead ended, and multiplied. Maybe that's the way the brain works when you don't understand things. Maybe that's what happened to the old man at the airport. Maybe we all share nightmares like that, noble sentiments and excuses. But it's a nightmare he can't escape. Maybe that's what Lucque meant, *le Point Vierge.*

He wrote three times during the year that seemed like a recovery from a bad wound. He told her about the Lincoln Memorial, and the Georgetown waterfront, and Dupont Circle at night. The second time he said he missed her most when he was in New York and saw Tony Randall leaving the Cartier store near St. Patrick's Cathedral after a private showing, and watching Jackie Kennedy by herself leaving One If By Land after an early reservation. The last time, he wrote about buying chocolate peanut butter cups at the small shop that specialized in pralines in downtown Fair Hope. He said he would have enjoyed rainy afternoons on the eastern shore of Mobile Bay with her.

He knew her response would be in long hand. And she would enjoy waiting for his next letter. But she never responded.

Madoff parted his lips.

"What's next? Plans?"

"Maybe Wisconsin, for a while," Lockett said.

Madoff stood. They walked to the door.

"Jung once said that inside every alcoholic is a seeker who got on the wrong path. You are fortunate, you touched each other again. Call it your posthumous life.

You had more precision the second time. You should be grateful, it's a light that never went out."

He extended his hand.

"You have my best wishes. Accept your days gently."

Outside the wind picked up. The western sky moved the same prairie clouds that fed tornados in late summer. Lockett thought about his doubts a month earlier, and what Emma said: "You had reason for optimism once. There is honor in replacing one hope with another."

Steinem put her hand on Lockett's knee.

"What's important is to understand the mistakes, the accidents, the faith you had, the one you loved and who loved you. You are your choices. They've taken you where you needed to go. Find a way to write about that commotion in your heart, that's who you are."

They left for separate terminals.

Nearly three decades after rehab, Lockett entered the November of his life. Sometimes he thought about Socrates who had asked, "Is life better at the end?" He smiled at the idea that for the last four or five years Santa had become more generous because he thought this would be Lockett's last Christmas. And at getting old, the hearing aids, the cataracts, the mirrors that showed him grey as a badger.

If nostalgia meant remembering passion, and regretting when it was gone, and if, like some said, after seventy you weren't relevant any more, then he was guilty. He had learned to live with that.

He knew he could have done some things better. But he had moved on. Memories had become treasures. He knew he had tasted more than most. He wouldn't die believing he had missed much. Other things happened now and he just cared less. Some things hadn't changed. He still preferred the company of women to men, and Louisiana in August to Wisconsin in January. It didn't make much difference where he went next.

He still carried her picture in his wallet instead of sticking it in some box and explaining to someone one day that the picture and the stories were never just a picture and stories. Whoever took the 1957 cheerleader photo captured her smiling wide with her arms out stretched in the purple and white uniform.

When he thought about growing old with someone it was always with her.

For ten years, part of what he enjoyed were visits to Grand Lac. Each time the city reminded him about their days together, as if to say, "I kept these toys to give them back one day."

The Hammond Avenue Presbyterian Church building had become an art center. The Cathedral was still there, long and grey and quiet. Both had required a bigger spiritual commitment than he'd been willing to make. But between the two, he had caught a look at God's peace.

In December, a year ago, just after dark, Lockett stood under a bright light across the street from Molly's house, like an old ghost who had never left the neighborhood. He looked for a long time as if to see their young hearts one more time. He felt the same north wind that fed itself through the narrow space between the two houses at her back door where they shivered and laughed and mocked ideas about ever needing to be anywhere without each other.

The house had been well cared for. The front porch was enclosed with thermal windows. A large apple tree in the front yard had replaced a crabapple and two others in the back where fireflies blinked in damp grass before the new garage. He noticed the seven foot dried hollyhocks he had taken for granted next to dormant hydrangea and cut down peony bushes on the side of the house where Fats had parked. He pictured the softball sized crimson flowers that were young with her. He imagined they sensed something important was gone after she lived there and loved and moved away.

Lights were on in her room on the second story in the back. He thought about the father she loved so much who brought her there to be hurt. He could almost hear the portable record player and the music she played in her room, the Four Freshmen, Glen Miller, Johnny Mathis, songs that seemed to define what it meant to be young and alive. He smiled at the way the lyrics became part of who they were to each other. Sometimes he didn't finish his thoughts.

The sky seemed waiting for a rain on the overcast morning last spring when Lockett walked the eroded beach near Dutchman's Creek. Winds and rain had wiped out the birch grove. He thought about the garden behind the wall she had mentioned. He imagined them together in the middle of flowers and paths and patterns that varied, maybe holding hands, like the quiet circles around the skating rink, maybe enjoying the scents. He knew he felt more than he was admitting.

A large, almost white driftwood log was partially buried in sand about twenty feet from the lake. He sat for thirty minutes looking at the water. It seemed natural to be back and alive. He thought of their time together that had been all used up, time to accept the eleventh hour and his own death.

He listened to an early robin sing as if it knew something special happened here, what Thomas Merton had called, "the feeling of one note above all."

In that special stillness he talked to her and said thank you.

The rain started.

Three years earlier, it had come out of nowhere.

"Cervical cancer," Cloutier said. "It was a while ago. I remember the leaves were red. You were in New York or someplace. You guy's went steady, right?"

Lockett choked back a tear.

To have called the cancer "bigger than ourselves" was how much she had regretted and cared at the same time. The fall had always been her favorite time of year. Maybe she had just put down a book of poems and fallen asleep.

No good thing ever dies.

For several days, he spent time by himself on Grand Lac's north shore. She would have noticed the male birch that had blossomed enough to fertilize nearby female trees. And enjoyed the people with accents who counted the days in each season like the Heino's.

"Write," Steinem had said.

Molly would have liked that idea.

"When all the world is young, lad,
And all the trees are green,
And every goose a swan, lad,
And every lass a queen;
Then hey for boot and horse, lad,
And round the world away!
Young blood must have its course, lad,
And every dog his day."

"When all the world is old, lad,
And all the trees are brown;
And all the sport is stale, lad,
And all the wheels run down;
Creep home, and take your place there,
The spent and maimed among;
God grant you find one face there,
You loved when you were young."

Charles Kingsley, *Young and Old*